Where Were You In The Beginning

Eunice Kim

 www.trafford.com
North America & international
toll-free: 844-688-6899 (USA & Canada)
fax: 812 355 4082

Contents

Preface

Where were you in the beginning? This eternal question led me to contemplate who I am and my link to the outside world. One night, while observing nature, the moon, and stars, I realized that I belong to the cosmos, in the same space as other stars. I recognized a connection between my life and the whole universe, that I am part of and function within this big universe; I am an important member of the universe, moving together in one celestial space. I am the true activity of the big existence and the larger order.

As I realized my existence as a part of the universe, I felt the invisible energy of creation from the beginning of the universe is still alive in me just as it exists in the petals of the flowers, in the trees, mountains, the sun, moon, and stars.

I've come to understand that my existence is not transient but infinite like those stars in the universe; my life is not worthless, but precious. Then, with that realization, I've regained my willpower to overcome fear, despair, and darkness. I recognized free will, the power of creation, and the light that the creator had initially given me.

This book is a story of finding ourselves through the characters' psychological and philosophical dialogue. I hope that through this book, young and old people worldwide see the true value of their existence, their importance, their preciousness, and their light.

Eunice Kim

About the Author

- Natural Philosophy, Nietzsche's Philosophy, and Biblical Philosophy Scholar
- Author of "To Victory! - Let There Be Light and Darkness" – published in 2017
- New Writer Literary Award for Fiction from the World Association of Literary Artists in Korea, 2000

Part 1: I, David

Chapter 1: Humiliation and the Temptation of Suicide

"I hate you, David! Don't you ever come near me again!"

Annie's pretty face distorted as she spat those bitter words. Her lips trembled violently like a fish hanging from a hook. Shaken, I collapsed in front of her. I wanted to say something, but I was frozen. Her harsh words branded my heart and I bowed my head like a sinner waiting for his punishment.

She gave me one last look as she ran away. I watched her leave then buried my face in the ground, trying desperately to stifle the wailing in my heart.

"Annie, my love, please don't leave me!!!"

I met Annie two years ago in my philosophy class. I enrolled in it because I was a philosophy major, but many non-major students took the course too as a general credit.

As always, I lounged in the back of the classroom and observed the other students who entered. I thought about the countless number of people that must have passed through this classroom, all of them studying, chatting, laughing, and squabbling. Despite these similarities, they all acted so differently. Some students looked simple, cheerful, and playful; while others looked serious, sad, and tense. I pondered what made us so different.

My daydreaming was interrupted when a tall professor with a nicely trimmed beard walked in. He immediately began his lecture on Nietzsche's philosophy, a favorite subject of mine. I perked up and corrected my posture.

But at that moment, my eyes fixated on a girl sitting in the front row. She was just my type: long hair, calm composure, and a mysterious charm. I tried to pay attention to the lecture, but my thoughts processed only her.

I remained in my seat when the lecture ended, hoping to catch a glimpse of her face. Finally she got up, organized her books, and turned towards the door and me. I saw how beautiful she was and my heart began to swell ecstatically. She looked much more mature than the other students, with a voluptuous body and confident gaze. Her snow-white skin, full lips, and large eyes mesmerized me. She walked slowly and gracefully out of the lecture hall. I found her every movement seductive. I only saw her for a moment, but she had a profound effect on me.

As I walked out of the classroom and was embraced by warm sunshine, the blowing wind played with my hair. I felt like a kid again. It was love at first sight.

Since that day, my habits revolved around her. I was the kind of person who would sleep during lectures and neglect my studies, but I started looking forward to going to that one class. It meant I could see her again.

Finally, the awaited day came. I went to the lecture hall 30 minutes early and settled where I could see her seat. As the time for lecture to begin drew near, I started to get anxious. The classroom was almost full and she hadn't yet arrived. I even got up from my seat and looked around to see if I had missed her, but she was nowhere to be seen. I took my jacket off and used it to save the seat next to me, just in case she was running late. Eventually the professor came in and started his second lecture on Nietzsche's philosophy. Today's specific topic was: *The Birth of Tragedy.*

Unable to find her even after the lecture began, my heart was heavy with disappointment. But just then, the door opened and a girl darted into the lecture room. She quickly scanned the room for an empty seat, her eyes wide like a scared rabbit. Unthinking, I stood up and gestured at the spot I was saving. She took my offer and sat next to me. I pointed out the textbook page we were studying, my hands trembling a little. She thanked me in a timid voice; I was intoxicated by the fragrance of her hair.

A few days later, I saw her again at a café in front of the school. I froze just like I had the first time I laid eyes on her. I watched her, dumbfounded, as she tucked her bangs behind an ear. One of her friends leaned in close to her and whispered just loud enough for me to hear, "Annie, look at that guy staring at us. He's stunned, just like the rest. Ha ha ha!"

She shot a glance over her shoulder at me and shrugged, looking uninterested. Too shy to approach, I sat near them and listened to them chat and laugh at some inside jokes.

After a fragment of time passed, she and her friends finally waved goodbye to each other and left. As she walked alone, I followed and considered how I could approach her. A few steps later, she turned around and asked playfully, "Are you following me?"

I was startled, but composed myself, acting cool.

"Why are you following me?"

"I'm not sure. May I accompany you for the walk?"

She watched me shuffle there awkwardly and hesitantly before silently joining me. My heart pounded with excitement and nervousness. I was speechless. Eventually we arrived in front of her dorm. Just as she was about to walk inside, I courageously asked, "Would you like to have dinner with me?"

She scrutinized me thoroughly from top to bottom and reluctantly said, "Okay."

Six months from that day, she was my sweetheart. She gave me many first experiences and made me feel things I had never felt before.

I followed her all around campus, to cafes, and everywhere I could to protect her. When I walked on campus holding her hand, I took pride when I noticed the envious eyes of the other male students.

In our relationship, she was the queen bee and I was a drone willing to die for her. She was a gorgeous rose and I loved her sharp thorns. She awakened me to a path of love, a world of sensuality, filled with all kinds of secret adventures and pleasures. For a while my heart was confused as to whether I was on the path to true love. My life used to be simple, but nothing was simple anymore.

Gradually, I was overwhelmed by the flood of expectations, desires, and hopes gushing through my heart. I melted at her touch and floated at the sound of her voice. She was my siren, my Eve, offering me her forbidden fruit. I abandoned myself to her: to absorb her and feel absorbed by her completely. Never in my life have I loved anyone as fervently as I loved her.

During the day I resigned myself to her touch, always begging for more. At night I saw private screenings entailing my most secret fantasies of her. Waking up in the middle of the night in ecstasy then going through the morning with tired, hungry eyes began to take its toll on me. The innocent, childlike quality of my soul was eroding as my adult self was born into the world. The philosophy books that once interested me were of no use. Everything else was insipid except for my desire for Annie.

It was a beautiful day without a cloud in the blue sky. She and I were lying on the quad, reading books. The garden in front of us was full of fresh roses. She smiled more magnificently than any rose and said, "It's pretty!"

I asked, "Would you like me to cut it for you?" I wanted to do whatever her wish was.

"No. Don't. So, others can also share the pretty roses and feel happy."

At that time, I truly believed she was an angel from heaven. She was a flower and I was the honey bee circling the flower for sweet nectar. I wanted to express my love for her. So I hugged Annie and said in a serious tone of voice, "Annie, I came to this earth to meet you! Nothing can separate us! Let us love each other until we die!'

I wanted to confirm our relationship, but Annie said nothing. Her silence disturbed me. I hugged and caressed her so I could dispel my anxiety; unable to read her, I fell into a more bottomless bog of anxiety and panic.

As the season changed, the autumn wind cooled our relationship and slowly a gap in our relationship emerged. As time passed, she acted suspiciously and became distracted. While talking and drinking coffee with me, her eyes hung in the air. Even walking together holding hands, hers had no energy. Her smile was faked with burdened production. Her words lost meaning. Each one took a great struggle and came only haltingly, through tired lips. She began making excuses.

"Today I have a lot of homework."

"Today I have a headache."

"Today I must meet a friend."

But I had to know why she was acting strangely. I had to renew our relationship before it was too late. So I came up with an idea of going on a trip together. To make money for this imagined trip, I worked many part-time jobs until late at night. After I saved ample money, I mentioned to her carefully, "Annie, I want to take you on a trip."

She paused, flashed her eyes, and said, "Well, anywhere I can go shopping should be okay!'

I was instead thinking of going to a beautiful beach or mountain cabin rather than shopping. But I quickly agreed with her, afraid of her changing her mind. *Wherever Annie wants to go, I am content.*

On the day of the trip, she wore a luxurious, oversized, floppy-brim hat and shiny sunglasses. I was filled with happiness and pride as I became her partner.

We drove along the highway that stretched along the sea, inhaling the fresh air. I loved watching white clouds drifting in the blue sky, geese flying overhead, Annie's hair fluttering in the wind, and her delicious laughter. Today the world was beautiful, friendly, and on my side. I said merrily, "Isn't the world beautiful, Annie?"

She replied in a challenge, "But if we were driving a sports car right now, don't you think the world would be even more beautiful?"

My used car rattled defiantly. I tried to look unfazed as I said, "You think so?"

"Of course! You can't fully enjoy this beautiful world if you are poor."

My fearful heart concentrated on her words, but I told myself: *Let's think later. For now, let's enjoy this moment.*

We arrived in a city of splendor and abundance. Annie was thrilled by the extravagant atmosphere and I relished the sound in her melodious voice. She looked adorable overcome with the excitement of spending on exorbitant things. She kept buying and taking. She seemed ignorant of my poor financial condition. I felt uneasy following her, carrying shopping bags in both hands. As my saved money dwindled, I became more anxious and sensitive, sweating from my forehead. When I hesitated at the next cashier counter, she asked me annoyed, "What's the problem?"

"It's nothing!" My face reddened and my heart wobbled like jelly.

We went into an expensive looking restaurant for dinner. I ordered wine to create a romantic atmosphere and made up my mind to propose to her tonight. After we clinked our wine glasses, I said earnestly, "Annie, I love you; I want to be your lifelong companion!"

"Do you have a career plan that will provide me with a happy and comfortable life? Well?"

Her question took me aback, but I tried to maintain nonchalance. To be honest, I was completely hopeless— without a goal in life. "I haven't thought about it yet. I'll plan with you in the future."

She gave me a sarcastic look and passionately discarded her wine glass on the table so that some of the wine spilled out the rim.

"You mean you don't have any plan for your future, such as getting a job or planning your own business and gaining material wealth? Then you don't have any clue how you are going to provide me with a comfortable life? Or... are your parents rich?"

Annie observed me for a moment. When she saw me bowing my head without any response, Annie threw a napkin on the table and exclaimed, "Oh this is grand. You have no wealth to inherit, no idea of your future, and you expect me to commit myself to an incompetent person like you? This is degrading. I want to leave. Now!"

Trembling with anger, she stood up and walked out brusquely. I felt deeply wounded as though she had plunged a knife into my heart; I wished to kill myself to stop the stammering embarrassment.

After we returned from the trip the cracks began to expand in our relationship. Her unquenchable desire and ambition showed us that we were different. It was clear that she was preparing to leave me. Everything began to collapse inside me.

She began to show blatant dissatisfaction with me and openly ignored my presence by meeting other male students. She was like a female bird searching for a male companion who could provide her the biggest, fanciest nest. She was even unapologetic in her cheating. I couldn't think of a way to stop it. I felt invisible.

How can I satisfy her? I have to find a way to satisfy her somehow!!! No one else can have her! I must get rich to keep her. But how?

The next day, as always, I waited for her outside the classroom. She saw me and said with utter contempt, "I'm busy right now."

She built barriers that I couldn't cross, but I couldn't give up on her. So the next day I waited for her outside the classroom again. The moment she saw me, she grumbled in a voice full of hatred and contempt through her firm, narrow lips, "David. Stop being childish. I don't want to be with you anymore. Let's end this now."

Then, without giving me a chance to speak, she ran. Remaining behind, I stared at her running figure. I was shaken to the roots of my being. Other students who witnessed the incident whispered among themselves. I was totally humiliated in front of the other students and our friends. Ashamed, I ran holding my crumpled pride and scolded myself. *You stupid coward!*

I tripped mid-sprint and fell into some passersby. I stumbled further into the street and caught my reflection in a shop window. I stopped and pointed at my pathetic self. Then I screamed, "You fool! How come you never thought about your future?"

I slammed the brick wall with my fist. My face was smeared with pain and tears. To avoid attention, I wandered away, not knowing where I was going. Concrete turned to sand and before I knew it I had arrived at the beach near campus. The ocean waves crashed violently against the shore, shooting ripples into my soul. I did not know what to do with myself. Her voice of hatred and contempt rang louder than the waves. I wished I could be carried off by the water and have all my shame washed away. So I walked into the water, even as the ocean pushed back against me. I stumbled, chin-deep, and let the air escape from my lungs. I wished to rest there forever.

Something dark and muffled called out to me. My lungs burned as I swam against the waves, towards the voice. I thought I saw Annie stretching her hands toward me and beckoning, "David, come closer to me!"

Her shiny black eyes stared at me passionately as her long hair swayed gently in the ocean breeze. She stretched her arms rhythmically, welcoming me. I could feel my heart soar as my body sank toward her.

"Come closer! Closer..."

I thrashed my limbs with all my might. The closer I got, the farther the waves carried her. Annie's moist, red lips, plump like ripened cherries, mouthed my name. With a final push I outstretched my hand and grabbed for a lock of her fluttering hair, but then my body started to cramp. The last bit of air escaped me and I choked as my vision blurred.

When I woke up, I was lying on the sand surrounded by people. My hands were clutching seaweed. Someone in the crowd began explaining to another that it looked like a suicide attempt. A man saw me sink into the deep water and jumped in to rescue me.

I was so embarrassed that I considered actually killing myself. I brushed the sand off and got up. Concerned people asked me to wait for the ambulance, but I just thanked them and shuffled away before causing a bigger stir.

The next day I sat curled up in my room, searching for a solution to Annie's puzzling heart. I heard two inner voices quarreling about the situation. One of them said, *Let's respect the life she wants and accept that our time together was just a beautiful memory.*

Then I heard another voice rebelling, *No, I can't let her go! Annie is the love of my life. I have to keep her by my side forever! I can't let her go to anyone else!*

The two voices echoed in my head, confusing me. And the more I felt confused, the more I missed Annie. I rushed out of my room and ran to campus, looking for her all over as though I followed some dark calling. But she wasn't anywhere.

After a while, my sanity returned to my exhausted body. I took a moment to sink into my own thoughts.

Annie was always by my side, but where is she now? Why am I wandering alone? Why do I have to be miserable, distressed, and sad?

Around me, students were running around in a hurry, carrying heavy backpacks. I laughed a small, derisive laugh at myself, thinking, *Other students run to their classrooms, but I run to find my girlfriend.*

My thoughts were interrupted by someone shouting. I looked across the street and saw the old homeless man who wanders the campus muttering to himself while clutching his Bible. I couldn't make out what he was saying so I walked to avoid him entirely. *That old man must be crazy!*

I spent the next several days becoming obsessed with my search for Annie. Although she left me, I never let her go in my heart. Ever since she left, the void grew bigger and darker each day until everything felt like it was cast in shadow.

For the rest of my college years, I experienced the unending inner turbulence. I hung around her, watching her flying hither and thither and finally flying freely away from me. My longing for Annie turned into obsession and eventually became a hindrance. Every night, I sought Annie in my dreams. At least in my dream, I could be with her and she was mine. In the morning, I was afraid of waking without her. I hated the morning light that gleamed on my eyes through the window, scattering her ghost. So I quickly got up, pulled the curtain closed, and leapt back into bed to maintain that phantom of Annie. Even after I closed the curtain, the light still penetrated my room. Beaten, I covered my face with the blanket and called upon Annie to come to me.

After a while, she appeared in my sleep, urging me to come closer to her. "David, come closer to me. Closer. Closer..."

I entered a state of ecstasy. I obeyed the momentary impulse to follow her, calling her name excitedly, "Annie!"

Surprised by my own loud voice screaming, the illusion began to slip. I tried to grab her, desperate to cling to the image, "No! No! Stay the same!"

I shut my eyes tightly and concentrated on the pain that her mirage left me. Finally she appeared again, whispering, "David, come closer to me. Come closer. Closer."

Determined not to lose her this time, I dashed towards her. Time seemed to stretch as I reached my hands for her. At last, I was in her arms. She brushed my forehead with her lips. I was helpless, and I begged her in a trembling voice, "Annie, just like this. Stay by my side forever."

"Do you want me that much?" I nodded.

"Okay. Then follow me," she said in a commanding voice.

Her grip around my hands tightened and her skin began to change. I watched in horror as the beautiful features of her face began to morph into a cloud of dark smoke. I heard her laugh mockingly as the smoke formed the slightest hint of a wicked smile. "Hahahaha! I don't want to live with you, David. But if you died, maybe we could be together."

Then she started walking, holding my hand firmly. In the darkness, a barely lit cave appeared. I was terrified, but I couldn't bring myself to let go of her hand. *As long as she is by my side, I must endure any fear.*

In the murky cave, there were people resembling me. They stared at me with obsessed, lost eyes. Annie sat at the center like a queen among them. She let me sit on her lap. I absolutely became hers, and I was terribly happy. As soon as the people resembling me witnessed this sight, they raged like crazy, staring at me with jealousy and contempt. My soul cried out in a swamp of pleasures, *Oh! My love, Annie!!!*

An unpleasant buzzing shook me out of my pleasure. The phone ringing on my nightstand was going off. I opened it and read the text message.

[News from the Alumni Association – 7PM tonight, Annie's wedding at the Student Union Hall]

At that moment my brain began to scramble. I grumbled in total confusion. *I was on her lap. But...what is this message?*

As my mind raced, I could feel Annie's fingers slide through my hair. I reread the message over and over again.

[News from the Alumni Association – 7PM tonight, Annie's wedding at the Student Union Hall]

Bewildered, I tried to calm myself.

Don't worry about anything! Annie is by my side right now. This is where she and I can be together forever. Isn't that what she said? That she'd live with me if I died. Maybe this is a place after death... No, it can't be! I'm thinking and feeling in the present. Then, what is the meaning of this message?

I was uncontrollably devastated and angry. I called her name, my voice piercing the ceiling. A cool, pleasant memory passed through my head.

"Annie, where are you? Come closer to me."

I waited for her to reappear. The desolate stillness felt like a fog in the room, until finally she emerged. "David, I'm here."

She appeared in a white wedding dress. Filled with rage and loathing, I turned into a ferocious beast. I gripped her and threw her on the bed and started taking off her wedding dress. She did not resist. My hands trembled fiercely in violent jealousy. Finally, her white body was revealed.

"It's almost done. Let's finish this now. Annie, I love you. I love you."

I embraced her with both arms and began to force her. She didn't even move.

"Annie, I love you. I love you. Please, answer me. Say something!"

She did not respond until the end. I put my hands around her neck and slowly began to choke her to death. Fear and that familiar mystic, transitory pleasure arose within me. I yelled, "Let's die together!"

"Why?" She looked at me with an expressionless face, questioning my exclamation.

"Because I love you to death."

"But, why should I die, too? I don't want to die!"

"No! You must die, too!" I won't let you live with another man!"

"No, I don't want to!" she yelled, fearing death.

I choked her harder and harder. Death was the only solution for us. At the bottom of my mountain of fear and anxiety was a black hole filled with ecstasy and bliss.

I awoke from my dream to the cold wind blowing through the window. I opened my eyes, trembling from the chill. My blanket was thrown out at the bottom of the bed, and my pillow was soaked wet with my sweat.

Outside, the sky was black repose. Everything was frozen in deathly silence, save for the occasional wind that brushed past my window. Lying in my bed like a corpse, I drank the cold, thin air of the autumn night and said aloud, "That was the worst nightmare I ever had."

Chapter 2: Dreams and The Birth of Tragedy

I have laid in my bed for a few days without eating. I loathed the fact that I succumbed to the world to ease my hunger and suckered people into liking me. Ever since I separated from Annie, I have remained alone in my room. I felt that I did not fit into the community of others any longer. I was afraid of meeting with people; I was always preoccupied with my thoughts. I was disgusted by the people who rejected me, anguished by the melancholy in my heart, and felt bitter hatred against the world and myself. My soul grieved the person I became. I had trampled on everything! I felt like I became a black sheep in my family, the promising son who has gone astray, even mad. I isolated myself and disconnected from my friends, my family, and the world.

In my room, I closed my eyes and waited for my imagination to emerge: avoiding reality and escaping to a temporary haven because I only found solace with my ghosts. At night, I immersed myself in my dreams while I slept; during the day, I reached my haven by closing my eyes and envisioning what I wanted to see. I lived between imaginings and delusions. I often saw my beloved apparition with a clarity greater than reality.

Today however, no matter how long I tried, I couldn't bring forth the illusions. Impatient, I became irritated, my empty stomach growled and I couldn't stop thinking about food. Eventually, overwhelming hunger made me yield. I got up and frantically scavenged the freezer and ate vigorously. I felt crazy. I felt like weakened scum, allowing my stomach to command my mind.

With my stomach full, I regained a peaceful mentality. I thought something was definitely wrong with me; I knew this was not normal. I thought, perhaps, because of my lasting anxiety and obsession I was losing my mind. I felt the seriousness of my mental state and an urge to find resolution. I felt that if I allowed this sickness to hold any longer, I really was crazy. I had to free myself of something deadly, deep inside me.

There was also another side of me that just wanted to give up and die. Death no longer seemed scary to me. I simply did not have the courage to face the real world; I just wanted to run away from reality to my dreams. Pain was raging inside me: pushing, finding no way toward the light, toward reason. My soul was ailing. I closed my eyes and asked myself –*Was there anything left to live for?*

In the dense stillness, I marinated in thought; I searched for the answer. That's when a memory of a philosophy class came to mind. In particular, one phrase from *The Birth of Tragedy* shot like lightning into my consciousness. Friederich Nietzsche's philosophy on the dream realities says: "Here we enjoy an immediate apprehension of form, all shapes speak to us directly..."

Yes, this dream reality was mentioned in Nietzsche's philosophy. I tried to connect Nietzsche's dream world to the illusions that I experienced. I sought to examine my sickness by understanding the phantoms appearing in my subconscious mind – my dream reality.

Yes! This phantom I see in my sleep and in my awakened state is a mixture of images of my desires. In my dreams, I love; I hate; I am happy. I am strong and the world is on my side. In the delusion, my truth is accepted as the universal truth. Therefore, my dream was more desirable than the real world, and I preferred to live in my imagination.

In the real world, I am worthless, miserable, hopeless, and directionless. Above all, what makes me miserable and disturbs me is that I do not know the answer to the questions: Why should I live? What should I live for?

I am failing to sustain this meaningless life day after day. When I open my eyes in the morning, I feel unpleasant for no reason. I'm angry because I'm depressed and disgusted with myself and the real world. I despise everything. I'm afraid to meet people. I don't want to do anything.

I leapt out of bed and pulled the *The Birth of Tragedy* from the bookshelf and began to eagerly read with the vague expectation of finding a clue to my problem.

Nietzsche, in *The Birth of the Tragedy*, discussed the conflict and resolution of man's duality in the inner self: good and bad, pain and joy, self-discipline and disorder, rational thinking and sensational pleasure, and so on. Nietzsche described two different aspects of human nature coexisting within us: one is Dionysian, whose nature is sensual, spontaneous, disordered, emotional, and ecstatic; another is Apollonian, whose nature is rational, ordered, and self-disciplined. He also said that all these antagonistic apprehensions of form appear as ghosts and that, during this experience, one can either find and renew to be a stronger person or destroy oneself completely.

Of the two characters, I thought I more resembled the Dionysian. My resemblance to Dionysian was a dissatisfaction with the world lurking in my mind, doubts about justice and truth, and rebellion against the world and myself. This dissatisfaction was the cause of my struggle.

In my struggle, my heart is painfully contracted by dissatisfaction and fear, and at the same moment, I feel joy and ecstasy from rebelling against the world. And somehow the fear and joy are oddly mixed with one another creating hysteria or uncontrollable emotions. Nietzsche said that the periodical reconciliation of fear and joy in the perpetual conflicts of diverse characters within is the character of Dionysian.

In me, like Nietzsche said, there seemed to be two contrasting characters coexisting in my subconsciousness: one desires sensation, frenzy, destruction, and ecstasy like Dionysian and another wishing for order and self-discipline like Apollonia. Using Nietzsche's theory, I tried to further analyze the causes of my outrageous feelings and uncontrollable anger.

Although I wanted to bear the fruit of my love, it did not come true because I couldn't satisfy my lover's desires. I thought if we loved each other wholeheartedly our love would be complete. However, this love game was not as simple as I thought. My loved one forsook me because I could not satisfy her desires and ambitions. So I went through dark days with the irreconcilable pain and tears in my heart. I felt like she and the world had betrayed me.

My torn love left me with a deep scar of dreadful melancholy and frustration. This scar bred self-hate, self-isolation, and despair. I thought I could no longer bear this life. But more than with anything, I was disgusted with myself, who lacked the ability to provide what my lover wanted. Eventually, my anger turned to contempt for this world, which made me feel that life on earth is ugly and tricky.

Since I was incapable of facing reality, I lived in my delusions and subconscious hereby denying it. As a result, I was incompetent, lazy, and a coward.

As time passed by, my phantom disfigured. My anger began to take revenge against them. I was no longer a naïve innocent person; I turned into a degenerate who hurt and tortured other people for revenge. And I took great pleasure in being a sadist. The color of my dream was no longer light, but dark; I fought and competed against many demons for power.

Although I wanted to diagnose my symptoms rationally, I could not endure the frustration and anger raging inside me. Irritated and feeling suffocated in my small cage, I ran outside to the street. I wanted to talk to someone regarding my failure and torment, but I didn't have anyone to speak to. It felt like I hadn't spoken to anyone in a long time.

Feeling tired after walking for a while, I stepped into a small café where the interior was decorated in cozy lighting; a few people were drinking and listening to a sweet musical melody. To hide the appearance of abnormality, I sat in a corner seat and ordered a merlot, pretending to sing along and move along the rhythm.

When the waiter brought the wine, I gulped the entire glass in one swallow. The alcohol comforted my agitated heart, had an effect of loosening my stiff intensity, and complicated mind. It had been a long time since I felt relaxed. I wanted to keep feeling good and enjoy this intoxicated mood; so I ordered a whole bottle and drank and drank. Many different emotions surged as the intoxication seemed to give me the courage and power to do anything.

I looked around the café. My gaze stopped on the TV hanging above the counter. On the screen, it showed the animal world; a hungry lion with its fierce, roaring eyes was about to ambush a fawn, which had barely begun to walk, next to its mother. The hungry lion spotted the vulnerable, newborn deer, held its breath, and waited patiently for the right moment to attack; when the infant stumbled, the lion struck in a flash, biting the feeble neck of the baby. The fawn struggled to survive and then, losing its strength, collapsed its body sadly. The lion slowly began to tear the deer's flesh and devour it. Meanwhile, hyenas gathered in groups waiting for the lion to finish his meal.

I got indignant and felt nauseated. I felt that I was the baby deer, the lion with absolute power was the world, and the insidious hyena was society.

I looked at the people around me. Nobody seemed to show any interest in the TV. No one was angry at the scene of the poor baby deer. As I saw their indifference, I couldn't hold my anger anymore; I stood up and spat out colorful words at the person sitting under the TV, trembling as my face filled with rage. "Hey, man! Turn off that damn TV!"

At my sudden reaction, the people sitting next to my table grumbled. I turned toward them, shouting, my face reddening in anger, "What are you guys whispering about? You don't have any sympathy for that poor baby deer? Do you think it is okay in this society that the strong ones are eating the weak ones?"

One of the people sitting by my table responded with a laugh at my rude behavior. "Hey, drunkie, why don't you go home and sleep!"

"What? Who the hell are you to tell me what to do?" I yelled out erratically.

Eventually, I was kicked out of the café, dragged out by the employee's strong arms. The whole world became hostile to me and I was full of bitter hatred against everything and everybody around me. I was filled with a pulsing rage which erupted like lava out of me. I picked up a stone from the earth and threw it as hard as I could into the sky. The stone fell back down over my head and I felt blood flowing from my forehead. Reflexively, I touched my forehead and saw red on my palms. Although it was terrible, I felt a sense of relief from the suffocation. I began to laugh at myself and the whole situation derisively and irresistibly. "To hell with this world! Yes, I'm a bastard, Dionysian! Yes, I will live my life my way! Who gives a damn what this world says?"

I wished to live my way as these damn days without any purpose in life continued, but my empty stomach continuously begged for food. So, I finally got a job at the school library.

Although my basic needs for survival were taken care of, the mundane continued; I was destroyed little by little like a fruit nibbled by insects. Every morning, I mechanically got up, went to work, returned home, and went to bed. I repeated this cycle every day. There was no joy or sadness, and each day was dull and lonely. I wanted to be free from the routine; I wanted to chat with anyone.

Then one Friday afternoon, I met an old homeless man on my way home from work. I've seen him, hovering around campus, talking to himself, and sometimes asking an absurd question to students passing by. Most of the students thought he was odd, probably insane. Although I encountered him several times in my school days, I avoided him convinced that he was crazy.

The old man sat on a bench, reading something. When I passed by, his eyes met mine as he lifted his head. At that moment, my eyes were fixed on him; I approached and began to talk as I rudely sat next to him, "Don't you have any other thing to do? Why are you sitting here every day and sometimes throwing absurd questions at students? For what?"

Surprised by my vulgar attack, the fellow calmly sat for a moment, searching for a word to respond, and said thoughtfully, "Young man, you remind me of myself when I was your age. Tonight, I think I will have to think about your question."

I felt a bit sorry after his humble response, but the feelings were beyond my control and I continued to attack him in a rude manner. "Why are you wandering around the streets? Aren't you ashamed?"

The old man did not physically react to my rudeness, but he answered in a quiet, factual manner.

"Young man, I am grateful that you're taking an interest in me. I thank you. I guess I'm wandering around because I think I should do something before I die. Young man, what do you live for in this world?"

"I live because I am unable to die. Why?'

The elder heaved a deep sigh and continued, "You are angry at the world and yourself. You're even thinking of suicide, aren't you? What makes you so angry?"

"I am disgusted with myself and everything this world entails."

"Perhaps, your bitter hatred against the world comes from quarreling with a world that does not follow your will?"

I yelled at the old man, "Do you think this world is moving according to YOUR will?"

"Well I think this world is too vast for me to counter alone. My sole voice cannot move this vast world."

"So, you are lost in the world and wandering around the streets like a deserter."

"I guess you could say that. Although I am old, I suppose I am still agonizing about not being able to reconcile with the world."

"Doesn't that make your life a failure?"

Although he spoke calmly, it was blatant he was hurt. "Yes, my life was a series of mistakes and regrets. For many days, I wandered in the maze of light and darkness, good and evil, and love and hate. Nevertheless, I still wander around because I want to know why I came to this world and want to awaken my soul before life is over. I think of it every day and I fight to keep my soul awake and vigilant."

"I don't understand how an awakening of your soul will help you survive this cruel world," I said.

"I think if I wake, I can understand other people; and if I know others, wouldn't I get a broader perspective of understanding of the world as a whole?

"That is total nonsense! Why would I need to understand others and this existence? This is MY life!"

"Of course, there is no reason to do so. Your life is yours to live. However, my arbitrary thoughts aggravate me, not others. The barriers and yokes I create isolate me from the world and eventually fuel negative thoughts, which then make me fall into either pessimism or decadence," he spoke.

"No matter what, we're all going to die one day. So what if I am a little cynical and live arbitrarily? Damn it, I don't care!"

At this point, I closed my mouth, feeling scorned for getting angry at and insulting the old man. *Am I trying to find my salvation by confiding in him? Am I looking for some sympathy from him for my failure and loneliness?*

Undisturbed by my ruthless manner and hysterical condition, the fellow, with an inscrutable face of many deep wrinkles, said nothing and looked up into the sky.

I changed my tactic and asked him, anticipating his answer, "Do you dream at night?"

"Yes, and I travel to many places in my dreams."

"I also dream at night. But my imagination continues when I am not asleep through my demons. Having lived in this condition for a long period, now I have a problem of not being able to distinguish my visions and reality. I live more vividly in my thoughts with the phantoms. I'm there more than I'm awake; I prefer my dream world to reality because in my dream I am a strong, bold person, when in actuality I am not. In my dream my wishes are fulfilled when in truth my situation is pathetic. "I don't know exactly when, but from some time ago these illusions became vile and wretched. I turned into an awful person in my dreams. I torture other people and curse at them. I even killed others cruelly for power. When I wake up from a nightmare, I am exhausted and drenched in sweat feeling guilty for turning into a bad person. Furthermore, those same kinds of phantoms linger in my mind all throughout the day, torturing me. They zap me of health and energy. As my condition got worse, I doubted my mental health state. Why do you think I see these things at night?" I waited for a response, wondering what his answer would be.

The old man listened to me calmly, unruffled, then said, "Don't you think the visions you see are a representation of your imperceptible inner self? In fact, the German philosopher Nietzsche thought of dream life as a hidden important outlet for life in his *The Birth of Tragedy*. Likewise, wouldn't you agree that the phantoms you see in your dreams and real life are the expression of your will wanting to expose your subconsciousness to yourself?"

"Did you say Nietzsche's *The Birth of Tragedy*?!"

The second the old man mentioned Nietzsche, I spontaneously sprang to my feet, unable to come up with the first coherent word. I shook my head with a frown and thought. *Did this old man really mention Nietzsche's philosophy? Does he who wanders the streets, homeless, really understand Nietzsche's philosophy?*

In that moment, my heart stood between excitement and disbelief to find someone else interested in Nietzsche. I held a great turmoil of skepticism, yet mirth.

Quickly, I settled and sat down beside the old man again. My insolent manner completely changed; I became more civilized with him, no longer lounging diagonally. In a way, I was thrilled with the joy of meeting someone who I can talk philosophy with. I decided to put away my doubts about the fellow, for a moment, and calmly opened my heart to listen to what he had to say.

He continued speaking in a quieted timbre, "Have you read Nietzsche's book?"

"Yes, Nietzsche is a philosopher I respect. How are you familiar with his work?"

"When I was as young as you, I fell in love with philosophy. Through Nietzsche's philosophy specifically, I became aware of my subconsciousness and the duality within me," he spoke.

"What about our dichotomy as humans?"

"In my understanding, there are two natures living together. These conflicting natures always create a perpetual tide: they clash against each other, trying to persuade and draw me to one side. Good or evil, they are always seeking to test their influence over my will," the old man said.

"But when I want to become a good person, why do I sometimes choose evil in my dreams?"

"In my opinion, if you see yourself as a vile person in a dream, wouldn't that be a sign of your will trying to communicate something through subconsciousness?"

"Communicate what?" I asked impatiently.

"Showing you your bad side to make you want to prevent it from coming out." the old man said cautiously.

"Unfortunately, even in real life, I also behave poorly: jealous of my friends, wishing for their failure, and being thrilled when they are troubled. I have been like this ever since I became a loser- after graduation," I confessed.

"You are right! Regardless of will, unconsciously, I sometimes compared myself with others and felt inferior. I wished for this self-consciousness to disappear. When I saw another person's misfortune, I sometimes felt relieved. I believed these emotional changes were the natural, inherent, psychological aspect of man. My innate, instinctive, psychological changes resembled the four seasons. As the seasons changed according to the different colors of spring, summer, autumn, and winter, I believed my emotions and mental states also changed in unison," he said.

"But then, isn't it a sin to feel content at someone else's misfortune?"

"Young man, what is a sin? Who judges your sin? Fyodor Dostoevsky, in *Crime and Punishment*, said: "If he has a conscience he will suffer for his mistake; that will be punishment—as well as the prison.... the man who has a conscience suffers whilst acknowledging his sin." Rather than reflecting on one's own behavior, aren't we perhaps burdening ourselves with the many variations of sin and suffering created by man?"

Suddenly like lightning, I felt the shudder of understanding in the old man's keen observations. *How long has my soul slept until this moment?* I tried to keep my composure, stay quiet, and let the old man continue.

"I believe, within us, there is a sense of good and evil, which is our conscience; this conscience is different from morality. Nietzsche expressed that consciousness is the conflict of the Apollonian and the Dionysian: so as to say, we all have two souls which are constructive and destructive at the same time. For example, there are times when our anguish and hard times are comforted by beauty, the arts, or music. In this state of peace with inner self, my environment, and social order, I am an Apollonian. At that time, my soul preferred being content and dreaming of virtue. On the other hand, there are times when I want to lose myself in darkness: enjoy intoxication, mindlessness, ecstasies, and self-harm in the form of physical pain. When I am in this barbaric state, I am a Dionysian. At that time, I am in a dream state, my savage nature controls me and my toxicity implodes. In life, there are perpetual conflicts within us following this duplexity; they hardly ever reconcile with one another. And we sometimes mistake the uncivilized nature of human existence, Dionysian, as sin. But I don't think we can say this natural psychology of humanity is a sin, as long as the inner fight does not hurt anyone outside. My inner struggle is that my unusual, bizarre behavior makes me uncomfortable, and as long as it does not hurt anybody else or obstruct justice outside of me, I expect in this state to find a way to reconcile the different tendencies of my ever-changing soul. The possible reconciliation can be obtained by unceasingly striving to rationally manage my antagonistic souls of order and frenzy, lead myself with a positive mind, listen to my conscience, find the light from my dark soul. By doing so, wouldn't I acknowledge my wrongdoing and therefore have a chance to be better? However, my rational self is not always in control. When I feel frustrated with logic, I urge to destroy the rigid order."

The fellow helped me to see myself through his honest story and I felt seen and understood. I was a kindred soul to my elder.

"You're an old man. Do you ever have the urge to rebel like an adolescent?"

"Aha! That's a very sharp criticism! Although my body is aged, rebellion does not seem to get old!"

"Then, wouldn't you like to compromise with the world now and conform to a normal life?"

"Foolishly I cannot reconcile with the world, like oil floating on water. But this life will also have to end someday."

"Is it so difficult? Why can't you just end it today?"

"Yes, even today, I probably might be able to stop it all by taking my life. As you said, young man, I have also thought that the only solution is ending my life, for I see death as a release. I often think that I should take my life. However, I've never made a plan on how to do it because it is so scary to die."

His words stirred my heart and penetrated my soul. Although I had contemplated the temptation to die, I never really planned to take my life. Could that be, as he said, because I was too afraid to die, or was it because I wanted to live?

I wasn't aware of the departing dusk; I was lost in a conversation with an old man. Without knowing, I was attracted to his interpretations of philosophy and wanted to continue chatting. I felt a certain spiritual affinity with the fellow, like an aged parent. I wanted to share my empathy and hold his wrinkled hands, but I was too shy to do so.

Chapter 3: The Universe and Me

All throughout the night, I couldn't fall into a deep sleep. I kept replaying what the old man said. I felt like I found a strand of hope while searching for an answer to my questions. In contrast to my expectation, the talk with the old man was enlightening. The old man seemed to have melded his own philosophy based on wisdom gained from his life experiences. Something about his carefree lifestyle, his self-assurance, and solemnity stirred my heart.

Outside, the morning approached. The first horizontal rays of morning light glimmered on the window panes. Rather than trying to go back to sleep, I got up and headed to the beach, wishing to watch the tranquil morning tide.

When I got to the ocean, the sky was red with dawn all the way to the horizon; where sky and sea merged in bluish uncertainty, the ocean slept under a layer of morning fog. As the sun's rays glimmered in the dawn, the morning mist slowly dissipated like pulled curtains and the waves tumbled up the beach and broke against the rocks.

The torrent of sunrise light opened my eyes with the beautiful gray-blue sky as the background. The sun played the morning prelude by splashing the primary colors on a large canvas orchestrating the sky and sea. Stirred to the core of my soul, I watched the breathtaking colors of the sunrise, feeling the symphony of the sky on the sandy beach.

The luminous sun broke through harsh rifts in the clouds, filling the gaps in between and reflecting off the ocean. My eyes filled with tears of joy in the mood of earnest attentiveness as the glorious sensation of sunlight filled the somber beauty in that moment.

I watched the path of the sun rising until I could no longer see with my eyes that the yellow sun turned dazzling. My eyes were closed to the glitz, but a gleam of sunshine kept dancing on my eyelids. Briefly, I was totally absolved and overwhelmed by the euphoria. After waking from this ecstasy, I implored aloud, "My soul, please wake up from your darkness!"

For a while I was drenched in my thoughts when, I suddenly had the urge to hike a mountain to escape from my dark soul and gloomy past. I wanted to have time to think of what I discussed with the old man, suspecting that I found a clue to my predicament.

I requested a few days off from work and prepared to go on the backpacking trip. The next day, I left for the mountains, my spirit uncaged.

The place I arrived was Yosemite National Park. At the park entrance, giant trees stood tall like generals guarding the park, guns stabbing the sky; they seemed to alert me that I was in a different world.

I opened my arms wide and breathed in the pleasant smell of trees in early summer. I saw remnants of snow atop the mountain, the big rock that looks like a towering dome, waterfalls gliding between cliffs, fresh streams flowing in valleys, lakes mimicking mirrors, various trees in green meadows, deer fleeing through the forest, and thousands of pretty flowers.

I felt like I was welcomed into a new world that wanted me. My heart was joyous; I was awake in the arms of nature until late when I fell into a calm sleep.

The next morning, I awoke to the sound of sparrows chirping outside the cabin window. I opened it, inhaled the clean mountain air, and heaved out a sigh of relief.

Ah, I think I'll live!

The fresh air washed my turbid soul. Excited, I enjoyed a delicious breakfast and walked with lightened feet and good mood. There were boulders everywhere, each with its own distinctive shape. They felt like a symbol of eternity. I spoke aloud as I envied the rocks, "Will they always be there, even after generations of change?"

The huge rocks formed the high mountain and the waterfall falling from the mountain was scattered by the wind, creating a rainbow. Numerous beams of light danced on the rainbow and gently came down to sit on tree branches, petals, on the wings of birds, and on the deer's horns.

I was awestruck by the magnificent scenery and applauded the beauty of nature. *Wow. Wow. How beautiful nature is!*

The waterfall from the high mountain made a clear pond in the middle, then the water continued to flow downward, forming another below. The waterfall below the mountain continued to flow down, forming a stream. They looked strong, gigantic, dignified, and structured, following their inherent system. I felt like I also was a part of nature, feeling obligated to follow in unison. As I inhaled the fresh air, I thought, *What is this energy, this power that moves my soul? What unknowable order does nature follow in harmony?*

The transparent lake breathed quietly as it embraced the sky, clouds, and trees. I laid down on the shore and let the cool breeze play with my hair. Comforted by the gentle touch, my soul began to open to the outside world. I felt a strange energy flowing around me and was shielded by that aura.

What is this energy or spirit in the wind wafting around me? Where did their strange movement begin and where does it end?

Fallen leaves were thrown by the wind into my face. At that moment, more questions came to mind.

Are those fallen leaves dead forever, or do they come back with new lives in the spring?

How do the sun, moon, and stars in the sky and nature move harmoniously together?

What unknowable larger imminent order is nature following?

Are humans, nature, and the universe created accidentally?

When did the universe, the earth, and humans start existing?

Who can accurately answer these questions?

I couldn't believe that humans, nature, and the stars in the universe were accidentally created, nor could I think that everything was created by coincidence. However, I was unable to find any clues to these questions since there was no trace of evidence.

I wanted to know. I wanted to know about the principles of all these things; I wanted to substantiate the truth of how this world was created from the beginning.

Is there a creator?

Is the Bible's story of the creation of heaven and earth true?

I heard the story of the creation of heaven and earth when I attended a Bible study in high school. The story was intriguing enough to draw my attention, but I wasn't convinced that the creator is God. There were too many unanswered questions about God.

How can I believe in a God that I cannot see with my eyes or hear with my ears?

Who has ever seen God? If anyone has, when and where?

But despite suspicion, I secretly wanted to believe and confirm God's existence. While my mind was running a tug of war with doubt and faith, the words of Ernest Hemingway in *For Whom the Bell Tolls* came to mind. "There probably still is God after all, although we have abolished him."

I looked at my surroundings and thought, *Have I ever seen air, which is the source of all life on earth, with my own eyes? As I am alive breathing this invisible air, does God, the creator, also exist?*

The sun revealed its presence after changing its position over top of my head. The vertical rays of the sun lifted petal faces, dried their dew, and a haze rose to my eyelashes. The sun rejuvenated everything on the earth; everything alive under the sun moved diligently, as it stored daily energy and food.

I wondered, *Why are they working so strenuously when our lives might be as fleeting as a mayfly?*

They worked laboriously throughout morning, afternoon, into evening, and night. I wanted to ask again, "Nature, aren't you burdened to work tirelessly to survive?"

Unlike this rhetorical question, I was distracted, feeling hungry. Once the hunger took over, I felt like all of these thoughts were futile, dishonest, and meaningless.

I rushed to the restaurant and ate all that I could. Once my belly was full, I was content and relaxed. I exclaimed, "Oh, I think I will live!"

I yelled this exclamation this morning when I breathed in the fresh air. Although the situation was very different, the feeling of relief was the same.

However, for some reason, there was something distasteful about it. Although I observed nature in the morning and contemplated the universal question, I felt worse than a surviving animal distracted by my body's urge and need to eat.

Following that feeling, a different thought slipped into my mind. *Does my body also resemble nature by following the flow of life?*

In searching for the answer, I remembered the philosophy of reincarnation and transmigration from Eastern philosophy I learned when I was in college. Under the philosophy of transmigration, death is not the end, but the separation of soul from body; reincarnation is the abstract belief that when a person dies, his soul is immortal, starting a new life in a different body or different physical form. Although the ideas of reincarnation and transmigration were interesting, I did not find any facts or evidence supporting these thoughts. I wondered how they came up with these ideas.

I spent all day questioning myself about so many unanswerable questions while I observed nature. The sun was setting and dusk came to the mountains. After the sun faded, the moon came up over the cliff and cast light across the meadow, plants, brook, and tree branches. As the stars peeked through quiet clouds passing by wet and bright, they reminded me of my mother. She was pure as a girl and her explanation of nature was so naïve. Although I became an adult, I still think of a certain shining star in the night sky as a 'mother's star.' She said to me, "David, that star is mine! Does it have a name?"

"That's Mars. It looks huge and shiny since it is close to the earth now," I replied.

"I see. David, Mom will always think of you by looking at that star, even if you are far away." I missed my mother, who always thought her son was the best; but, I soon felt sorry because of how I turned out to be. As I watched stars blinking in the night sky, I asked questions, "Where were the stars during the day? Does anybody live on the stars? Is there anyone who daydreams like me of the stars?"

In my illusion, the Little Prince appeared. The Little Prince, who traveled to Earth from his little star, asked me curiously, "I am from another star. Which star are you from?"

While his question confounded me, the Little Prince disappeared, with my daydream, leaving me perplexed.

I kept looking at the beauty of the twinkling stars and asked more peculiar questions. "Am I a neighbor and mystery of the universe to those who live on other stars, too? Am I a part of the universe?"

In the dark grass fields fireflies appeared, lighting their green lights. I was complacent in the glimmer. The radiance reminded me of my innocent youthful years when I played with them.

A host of images emerged in the illuminating green light: a good boy, who loved to read fairy tales, an ambitious adolescent with hopes and despairs, a college student lost with too much freedom, days of passion, happiness, and obsession after I met Annie, the days in darkness after Annie left, Jane, who I met temporarily to avenge my broken soul but forgot, days of not being able to compromise or adapt to society, and finally days filled with dissatisfaction, rebellion, melancholy, and a wish to die. I sank into a reverie and became lost. As the memories of the past days plunged into my mind, I tried to look within with insightful and keen eyes. *How and why was I trapped in darkness? Where was my light?*

To me, my light was only the woman I loved, Annie. Once she left me, my light disappeared with her; I felt imprisoned in a dark prison cell and betrayed. I misunderstood that she was my world and was confused that she was not only my savior, but eventually distorted my light and I dove into darkness. I rebelled against and scolded the world for my anger against my Annie, who left me.

I questioned, "Why did I rebel with rage, declaring the world to be full of lies, rather than looking inward?"

Sadly and yet deeply moved, I heard my inner voice speak. *Although those past days were turbulent, passionate, saturated with unquenchable desires, and unbearably painful, they were also pure, loving, and beautiful. My experiences from those journeys provided me with a chance to find my true self.*

Slowly the thick fog that shaded my eyes cleared, an epiphany after a long sleep came to mind. My soul, trapped in the black, cautiously opened its door. Within me, there was a great strife between preferring to live in the sun and preferring to live in shadow. My head was dizzy. My stomach contracted. My blood was on fire. The bulbous lump of despair began to break into pieces, but refused to succumb and screamed in anger, "I am you! Don't you try to separate us! We will live together!"

I was shaken to my roots, resisting this last fight, I yelled out to the darkside, "Get away from me!"

I divided into two opposing souls and they fought vigorously for a long time without exhaustion. The part of me wanting to keep my virtuosity and purity cheered the good soul and the part of me wanting to keep my ego and greed cheered the vile soul. The two pushed and trampled each other; their fight lasted for a long time. Lightning and thunderbolts split the two. The dark soul, stricken, clenched its teeth and grumbled, "I can't die! I am merely resting for a while!"

Finally, my soul struggling in the darkness found a dim ray penetrating through a tiny hole; my soul walked toward the hint of light.

I felt like I was released from heavy chains that were binding and crushing; I nervously walked out of the dungeon like an infant learning to walk. I felt I had regained my freedom. When I awoke, I was standing under the moonlight and all life had fallen asleep. I felt peaceful and happy within my existence. In the night sky the round moon led the stars. My mother's star walked along, too, smiling and whispering, "My dear son, I am always with you, even if you cannot see me behind the clouds!"

As I reminisced about my mother, I felt enthralled, like finding an oasis in the desert; I drank the water of hope from heaven, earth, and nature.

Chapter 4: Nature's Perspective on the Creation of Heaven and Earth

I observed the heavenly bodies embroidered in the sky as I laid down in an open field on the warm, early, midsummer night. The radiating flickers hung on a net placed in the sky; they joined hands, creating a constellation. There were different shapes of constellations in the night sky. They resembled a goat, a fish, and a ladle; all stars created the unique forms of the zodiac.

Lying down in the field and staring absentmindedly, drowsiness slowly overtook me and I sank into the dream world. My body became lighter and floated like a balloon. I became a young child opening my arms wide and flying into the sky. Under my feet, I saw myself asleep on the ground.

As I floated into the air, I saw a staircase layered in the cloud. At the top of the cloud stairway, a puff resembling a crocodile slowly passed, sticking its tongue out.

After climbing the stairs, a vast wilderness appeared. That place was an endless sand desert, whirlwinds spun around. After passing through a sandy valley, a space filled with shimmering waves appeared. In that space, an aura of rainbow colors danced together in harmony, like the Aurora Borealis. Those colors were like the bars of light refracted by fragments of broken glass.

After passing through the space of sparkle, heaven appeared; small and large planets circled the earth. Some were reddish and others had rings around them, marking their atmospheres. Among them were some familiar, enormous stars that I learned about in astronomy class.

After passing through the celestial bodies, I followed some fascinating feeling calling out of the unknown; I reached a space filled with the deep silence of gravity. It seemed like this fascinating place was another sky above the normal sky. The place moved in silence with dignity and a godliness that I dared not refute. It seemed like a higher level of spirits resided here and I thought that this might be the place where gods and goddesses reside.

I awoke from a childish dream that I haven't had in a long time. Most of my recent dreams were wretched. I felt refreshed and pleasant, having a strand of hope that my youthful views were returning.

The new day began with beams of sun shining on all the creatures and pearls of dew on shiny leaves. The first rays shone brightly through the floating mist. Feeling content with the sun and earth, I climbed up a steep, forested mountain.

I inhaled the clean, sweet morning air, filled with joy, and walked into the wilderness.

After hiking a steep course, I found a stream flowing next to the trail. Tired, I sat on one of the stones by the stream. I washed my face with the cold water, dipped my feet in, and serenely gazed at the current. Below the clean water, there were clusters of smooth, shiny stones. They had unique patterns on their bodies - some wore wave stripes, some wore dazzling mixed colors, and some wore black and white spots.

Each pattern told where they started, their age, and how long they traveled down the river since they'd broken off of the big mountain.

I spoke to the stones, reading their designs like historical letters. "Stones! How long have you traveled alone from your mother mountain? For what do you travel and where is your destiny? Are those scars on your body telling of the hardships you've experienced on your journey?"

I talked to the current. "You, ever-flowing stream of water, how did you form, and to where are you endlessly flowing? What do you expect to find when you reach your destiny? Don't you ever get tired with the constant moving, not able to settle down? Or is there only advance, no retreat? Is my life a journey of constant challenges and an unknowable future, too?

I observed how the water flowed regardless of obstacles. Water found downward courses: through, around, under, or over. When an opportunity opened, water moved spontaneously; when stagnant, it rested in a state of ease and constant readiness.

I asked the creek, "Water, how do you adapt to all these obstacles in the world? How do you live with such nonchalance? How do you keep your tranquility? I should learn from you how to live. You don't seem to question much, but you take action trusting the flow of life. What is it that you trust? I want to know!"

I sat there amazed by how the stream flowed down endlessly. There seemed to be no end to the water. I kept thinking, *Where is the water coming from? From the top of the mountain, of course, but how did the water form up there? From rain and snow, obviously.*

I thought through the chain of events. The snow on the apex melted and became water. Flowing water found its way downhill initially, as small creeks. As small creeks progressed, they merged to form streams and rivers. Rivers eventually reached the ocean where water evaporated from the surface. Vapor was carried by the wind as it condensed into clouds and fell as rain or snow. Throughout the process, the water sustained all life, a never ending global process of water circulation from clouds to land, to the ocean, and back to the clouds.

"What a perfect program of nature! Who created this cycle? There seems to be a deeper balance that underlines nature. Is this system similar to Nietzsche's philosophy on eternal recurrence? Does this mean everything in the universe circulates, even humans?"

While I was immersed in deep thought, a frog jumped up from the rocks and sat on the grass. I was startled at first, but casually observed its body and bulging eyes. The frog greeted me in its croaking voice. I relaxed and replied, "Nice to meet you. Where are you from? Who made your swollen eyes for you?"

The frog showed off his unusual, long and slim, rolled tongue by demonstrating how he catches a fly from a wildflower. It made a croaking sound and behind the plant, I saw a bed of different flora.

I observed them up close and surprisingly, although they looked similar facially, each of the leaves had its own miniature detail pricked into it, like a delicate embroidery. They all had different, unique, intricate shapes and characteristics.

I asked them, "You, little flowers, who designed all your different shapes? For whom do you decorate yourself so pretty? How do you decorate the whole mountain with these little bodies?"

Above the flora, I saw a butterfly playing and dancing freely with the wind. Everything in nature moved and danced with changing circumstances and environment harmoniously with trust in the cycle.

Throughout the morning, I talked with bugs, fauna, birds, arbors, and plants, asking the same questions, "For what do you exist? For whom do you live?"

It seemed like there was some kind of interrelationship between nature and man. Like the shape of flowers were all different, people were all different. Like nature that wasn't going extinct, we, humans, also do not become extinct. I still wondered, "Is the continual existence of nature and humans a program of cosmic flow? Was this order created in the beginning? Who created this system?"

With many questions unanswered, I looked around nature once more and got up. I engraved their beautiful pictures in my soul; I walked with lighter feet than when I began.

As I was scaled down the hill, I left everything behind. The passing wind whispered in my ear, as if it was telling me a secret, "Oh! You, precious and great human being! The same Light that created you created us. Nature exists for you, for precious humans!"

Chapter 5: The Past and Reality

As I drove back home from the hike, I whistled and my heart rejoiced. Thinking of the journey of the past few days, nature had rejuvenated my soul. It cleansed my mind and loosened my anxiety. For the first time, my heart was overwhelmed with freedom that I hadn't felt for a long time.

I played the radio while enjoying the scenery. The music exalted and expanded my being to recognize the beauty of the outside world. A song I knew came out of the radio — "You Are Not Alone" by Michael Jackson. That song sadly and deeply stirred me as many forgotten memories welled up. I sank into a trance as my mind rewound.

It was one of the wandering and despairing days after I was deserted by Annie, a humiliating time that I would not want to remember. However, it was also the day of a new encounter with a forgotten person who awakened my soul. One incident after another, the past loomed in my soul.

It was a weekend just after the new semester began. The school dorm opened with a welcoming party for all returned students. On that day, I began to drink in the early evening, wishing to forget my terrible memories of Annie. By the time I joined the party, I was already very drunk.

In the party room, Michael Jackson's heartbreaking song shook the hearts of the guests. Students sang along and went to the dance floor, coupled. Drunken, I sang the song aloud, envying those dancing couples.

"How nice would it be if Annie were here with me?" I grumbled.

I knew that I was already drunk, but I didn't care and kept furiously drinking beer. As the alcohol went through my intestines, anger, which I tried to suppress all day, boiled up again, and I sought vengeance.

I looked around contemptuously and disdainfully. At that moment, the girl sitting at the table in front of me was staring at me. I approached her and asked, "Would you like to dance?"

I haughtily reached out my hand to the girl. She followed me to the dance floor, holding my hand without hesitation. Through her hand, I felt both kindness and affection.

At that moment, I had an impulse to caress her. I hugged her tightly and thought, *This girl may be as lonely as I am. Tonight, perhaps, we can comfort each other.*

She leaned her face against my shoulder; I could feel her body heat through her thin dress. My body burned with sensual thrills and curiosity. As her swollen breasts touched my chest, all my body piqued, my heart pounded and strained my breathing.

She absorbed the lyrics, yearning for love. I hugged her tight, stimulated, dancing slowly along with the music.

Within me, I was torn between two thoughts. The conflict brought up two distinct inner voices; these voices chimed in separate opinions as I lost self-control in excitement.

"If you sincerely desire her, then tell her your heart honestly and wait for her answer."

"No! You don't need it. She looks lonely, and wants you; think of Annie, who left for another man. You can take revenge on Annie by spending a night with her."

"No! Don't do anything irresponsible without love. Don't fall into temptation."

"What's so complicated about this? Nobody is watching and it is something we both desire. Just follow your impulse and be free."

"You know, even if others don't."

"Damn it! The righteous life that you've lived has been bothering you your whole life.

Your patience has been controlling and suppressing your natural emotions and desires; that is why you are angry right now. Accept what your body wants now.'

I agreed with the words of my rebellious inner voice and decided to accept the suggestion. I thought that, perhaps, this unruly personality was my true and natural self.

I hugged her more passionately, but heard a cry from my other inner voice, pleading with me to change my mind.

"Don't lose yourself to momentary temptation. It's wrong."

"Shut up! Be quiet! Listen to me! Tonight, her warm touch will soothe your aching heart. Then it'll make you forget the humiliation you received because of Annie."

"No! If you make one mistake now, you will continuously excuse yourself for making mistakes in the future and it will form bad habits."

"Stop with the tedious lecture. Life is about having fun and enjoying the journey since everything ends when we die."

Again, I thought he was right. I wanted to cast off the heavy burden of morality and live lightly, enjoying the pleasure of the world.

Not knowing my struggling heart, the girl I held in my arms moved smoothly to the music, leaning on me. I decided that I would take her to a quiet place when the music ended.

But that other voice was earnestly begging me, "Please, do not lose yourself. Don't fall into temptation, please."

"Don't interfere! Leave him alone. Let him live his life freely."

In my mind, the two conflicting perspectives fought fiercely with each other for their opposite viewpoints. I suffocated in the middle of their argument; feeling tired and nauseous, I struggled to get away from them. Just then, reality returned, as if pouring cold water on my back.

Again, I heard the sound of music and felt myself hugging the girl. Then, as the music ended, I released her and said the empty words, "Thank you."

I ran out of the dance hall, tumbling, unable to look into the girl's eyes, feeling guilty of my wicked thoughts.

The next day, I sat on a campus bench on a hill, trying to catch up on my studies; however, my effort was futile, I was unable to concentrate. My head was filled with fragments of many thoughts: worries, self-reproach, and bitterness. I heaved a great sigh. Distracted, I got up from the bench, finding a girl standing in front of me.

She greeted me with awkward shyness and spoke timidly, "Hello. Do you remember me?"

She smiled brightly, anticipating my response. I was stunned. I bluntly asked, "Do you know me?"

She blushed, her face reddening with embarrassment, and whispered, "We met last night at the party and danced."

"Oh... I am sorry. I can't remember last night. I was very drunk."

She muttered, "You left a deep impression on me."

I remained silent, not knowing what she wanted when she unexpectedly said, "I want to get acquainted with you. Can we become friends?"

Her words awoke a heavy blackness in my heart. The dark side of me suddenly gushed out, seizing that golden opportunity for revenge against Annie.

"This is it! Finally, my chance is here. Now I can get revenge on Annie by dating this girl. Isn't Annie dating a man in better condition after dumping me? Doesn't matter. I can show my friends that there are still girls who are attracted to me and rebuild my crumpled pride. My friends truly mocked me when I was broken. Oh! Heaven has not forsaken me!"

I answered her inquiry firmly and at once, "Okay. I think we can be friends."

Her name was Jane. She was sincere, truthful, and committed to me during every minute we met. However her innocence, dedication, and cute appearance did not stimulate me.

Through rumors and her friends, she already knew of my past relationship with Annie and understood the wounds and chaos. She accepted my pain and she patiently waited for it to be healed with time. She sincerely wanted to help me out of the swamp of despair, but I didn't need her help.

To me, all her sincere efforts were cumbersome because she was not attractive, gorgeous, or beautiful like Annie. Every day, Jane prepared lunch for both of us with all her care, but I was not interested in her. I ate the lunch stubbornly and mechanically and without gratitude. At that time, my attitude to her was like, "You made it because you wanted to. So I will eat it for you."

Although Jane was next to me, I saw a vision of hatred, prowling toward my unfulfilled love. Then one day, to execute the revenge scene I made up, I entered a café where

Annie often went, holding Jane's hand. Annie definitely was there. She casually glanced at Jane and sneered with judgment. Then she lifted her head triumphantly and chatted back to her friends, as if nothing happened.

Shaken to my heart in humiliation and disgust, I cursed myself, as I watched Annie's twisted smirk and laughter.

"Annie, I have been a fool for loving you." Unsure how to express my grief and anger, I clenched my teeth and frantically stared at the male students sitting around Annie. They also did not seem to envy me holding hands with Jane. Embarrassed by their dismissive attitude, I wanted to hide in a rat hole. And I blamed everything on Jane that this insulting situation occurred; she was nowhere near as pretty as Annie.

Unable to bridle my rage, I went off on Jane with my frustration and hate. "Jane, you humiliated me in front of my friends."

I shook off her hand, violently kicked the door, and ran outside. The next day, when Jane approached me with a lunch bag, I bluntly said, "Thank you for everything. Goodbye." And without looking back, I went away from her.

As I emerged, my cruel memories brought a new flood of tears to my eyes with infinite regret and chaos.

"Why am I crying in sadness?" Unclear of the reason for my sadness, I wanted to question my past, particularly the type of love that best revealed my truest self.

Annie, who I loved with my soul, was my pride. I loved her sensual beauty and provocative, arrogant personality. Her confident charm allured me and my desire for her blinded and pushed me into a swamp of obsession. I thought of her; she was a bog of pleasure and pain, where I could be happy and stay eternally. However, she didn't want me or love me. She chose another man and made me an incapable person, a loser.

I thought, *Was my turbulent love with Annie real love? Jane, who loved me sincerely, was the subject of my anger and yet a refuge. She was a symbol of truth and purity. However, her gentleness and thoughtfulness did not interest me, but rather irritated me. Yet, I needed her to reclaim my love. I used her innocence for my selfish purposes and when I did not need her any longer, I abandoned her. Why did Jane love me? What is the meaning of her love?*

I reevaluated the value of love by retracing the entire course of my romances. I burned all my soul for Annie. The only thing left for me was the black ashes. I used Jane; all that remained for me was regret and a chance to reflect. Why was I so selfish? And why am I regretting my past now? Why is my heart still aching?

I thought I had at least once thought about another person's feelings. Come to think of it, in the past years I never regretted or repented my mistake. I lived more aware of watching eyes. If I was remorseful, it embarrassed me. But now I ask, "Who makes me embarrassed? Who suppresses my repentance? Is my aching heart sending some kind of signal? Is it telling me not to live to impress others, but me?"

My chest stopped heaving and I thought as I looked at the blue sky through the car window, *Nature showed me my true self, taught me the wisdom of life, and helped me to look inward.*

I think I just finished the first stage of learning to walk through tumbling steps. Now, I think I will learn how to walk with better balance.

As I headed home, I self-soothed. I got off the highway as I approached campus. As I passed the school on the way to my apartment, a woman stood, head bowed, under a tree holding a bouquet. It drew my attention. It was the spot where the old man used to sit, muttering to himself. I saw many notes attached to the tree and the woman with her head bowed looked familiar. I was curious and wondered what was going on, so I slowed down and parked my car. I walked to the tree and the woman turned around. She left. As I watched her back from a distance, I trembled, feeling a longing agitation. My heart asked a wild question, "Maybe ... Jane?"

Under the tree was a white bouquet with a note. I read the note cautiously. "Goodbye my dearest friend, Ben. -Jane"

As I reread the note, my chest pounded under a massive wave of commotion. "Perhaps, you were the old, homeless man who walked around campus with a Bible under your arm, asking students absurd questions while you sat on the bench under the tree? Are you the old man who told me about your philosophy? Are you the old man who generously listened to my rebellion and struggle and humbly told me about your life? Your name was Ben? Then ... does this mean you passed away? And, you know Jane, too?"

I slumped to the ground, reminiscing about the old man I forgot. My heart was torn. So much of my past problematic, foolish, and inconsiderate behavior toward Ben surged in front of my eyes, causing agony and nausea. I was filled with hatred and I couldn't forgive myself for that insolent behavior.

I scorned, "How am I going to reconcile this situation? Now I cannot even ask for his forgiveness."

I sighed, cursed, and moaned, not knowing what to do. Frustrated, I looked up to the sky wrapped in a white veil; I saw a figure floating in the veil, smiling radiantly and cheerfully. I saw the generous smile of the old man. I wanted to cry as I reflected on my selfishness and ingratitude.

"Ben, you are still teaching me, even after you passed away. I will never forget you."

Part 2: I, Jane

Chapter 6: Little Angels

"Miss Jane!"

Seven-year-olds run toward me, raising their hands high in the air; I also run with my arms wide open and hug them. We missed each other during break.

"We missed you, teacher!"

"I missed you, too."

After I graduated college, I became an elementary school teacher because of how much I adore children. At school, I liked being close to the innocent youngsters because I had a chance to look back at myself, return to my innocence, and continue to grow with them. Through their sincere words and deeds, I met my younger self and it awakened my soul, the purity I lost.

I spend happy days playing, singing, and talking with elementary school lambs. Although they grow up in different home environments, they receive the same education in a designated classroom that teaches society and social life. And for kids there are times when it is not yet possible to distinguish between their home climate and the school climate. However, most angels naturally adapt to the new environment without any hesitation or awkwardness.

As the children study community interactions with their peers, they create their own unique culture and at the same time inherit the culture of the previous era. I also receive renewed energy and impetus from children. I teach children social skills and knowledge of the world, but the children show me the inherent nature and wisdom of human beings, the one that we are born with, and they make my soul mature.

I nickname them little angels, because the heavenly angels I imagine are like the little children of the world; every adult in this world was once a little angel when they were young. And I am sometimes still surprised by the fact that I am an adult when, in my heart, I am still a babe.

Among the angels who show me my younger self is a girl called Leah, who is smaller for her age. When it's time to play, she carries around a bear doll wrapped in a blanket on her back. The teddy bear's name is ET; Leah takes care of ET as her own brother. At lunch hour after Leah prays, eyes closed and small hands together, she talks to the teddy bear.

"ET, you must be hungry. I'll feed you something delicious."

She eats half of a cookie, gives the other half to ET, and asks, "Is it delicious?" Then she nods her head in joy, looking at the bear's face.

I reminisce about myself at seven years old and overlap the image of their happy faces. *Hey, Mongsil, are you bored? Let's play!* Mongsil was the name of the puppy that grew up with me. I grew up alone; Mongsil was my brother, sister, and friend. As a child, I talked and played with puppies and dolls. They understood my words and I understood their words, just like Leah.

There is a boy, Daniel, who resembles *The Little Prince*; he reminds me of my fantasy world. He has a delicate sensibility, poetic sense, and likes to draw pictures. When it's time for a break, he takes out a toy airplane, falls into his fantasy world, and makes the sound of an airplane flying, *whirrrr*, as he flies the airplane in his hands.

As I watch him play, I also fly into my fantasy dream world, which has been with me since childhood. It is my paradise, a garden of Eden, a resting place, built between the blue sky and the emerald sea.

I am curious about Daniel's goals, so I ask, "Daniel, what do you want to be when you grow up?"

"I want to be an airplane pilot and fly in the sky!"

"Cool! I also fly in the sky in my dreams."

"The feeling of flying is really fun!"

"Yes, it's very exciting!"

Daniel's dark and beautiful eyes twinkle as he speaks. In my eyes, I see Daniel flying through the infinite sky stretching to the end of the world.

There is also Scott, who always shows concerns for others. Scott has a naturally positive, bright personality, sometimes playful, and always likes to talk cheerfully with many friends. He volunteers to help weak friends and builds strong friendships. I ask about his future dream, admiring his innate service spirit. "Scott, what do you want to be when you grow up?"

"I will be a doctor!"

"What a wonderful dream! How did you come up with that?"

"I saw a kid who can't walk at the playground. I'm going to be a doctor so I can make him walk!"

I am impressed by the child's warmth and strong will. I appreciate his concern and care when he asks me every day how my days are going.

There is a boy named David, the same name as my previous boyfriend. David is always alone and quiet, either in class or during breaks. He does not express any particular interest in any subject or play. However, he sometimes looks pensive, sitting motionless, looking into the distance with a fathomless expression. I approach him, immersed in his daydream, and ask carefully, "David, what are you thinking about so hard?"

He responds, "Miss Jane, where did those clouds in the sky come from?"

My heart pounds at the child's enigmatic question. In his subtle expression, I see a man who was my melancholy, first love, who stole my soul and happened to have the same name as the babe.

On a bright and cheerful day of summer, I take the little angels on a picnic in an open field. I run after them with my arms fluttering like a butterfly. Feeling free outside, the children and I inhale breaths of fresh air. The clean breeze blows on our faces, gently stroking our hair, and exposing our foreheads to the sun. The sunlight and wind kiss us. The sunlight dazzles our eyes and the wind muffles our hair. Some of them tumble on the ground, falling on a small stone, but they get up. Without worrying about the wounds they continue to run and bounce gleefully, playing along with the natural elements.

A mother of a child who is watching us play calls to her youngster, worried, "Hey! Don't run! It's dangerous!"

That mother's voice reaches my ears through the air, and changes into the voice of my mother. *Jane! Always be careful! Mom is so worried about you!*

My mother has worried about me ever since my father suddenly passed away when I was in elementary school. Now that I'm an adult, I assure my mother that I am okay, looking at the blue sky. "Mom—I am an adult now. Do not worry!

.

After playing for a long time, we sit down on the grass under a tree and prepare for lunchtime. Leah, running around with ET on her small shoulders, says to me, "Miss Jane. My brother, ET, also came."

"Great! Welcome, ET! Nice to meet you! You must be happy having a good sister like Leah."

Leah, next to ET, says radiantly, "I like my brother, ET!"

"That's great. I also had a younger brother like ET when I was little."

"Really? Where is he now? I want to meet him soon!"

"His name was Mongsil and he was a puppy. He is in Heaven now."

"Where is Heaven? Is it very far? How can we go and meet him?"

"Heaven is in dreamland. If we go to dreamland, we can meet him."

"Then let's go now. I want to meet Mongsil."

"We can only go when we sleep. So let's wait."

"Yeah, okay."

I pull out a picture of Mongsil for Leah so that she can recognize him in her dreams. Leah grabs the photo of Mongsil with her two tiny hands and stares for a long time. I also look at Mongsil in the photo, feeling sorry that I haven't thought about him as I became an adult and whisper to him, "Hi, Mongsil. Let's meet in dreamland tonight!"

The children and I sit in a circle on the lawn and unpack our lunch boxes. Most bring food from home, but I hand out the meals that I prepared in advance for those who didn't. They look happy, eating their delicious lunches.

As I watch the children, I see David sitting in a corner. He could not focus on eating. With an anxious heart, I check David's bag. His lunch box is full of scrumptious food, made with care and devotion. The contrast between the hearty lunchbox and the child's indifference bring back sad memories. The sullen face of David, my first love, comes back and stirs my heart. The memory gushes forth.

When I was in college, I wanted to please my first boyfriend, David, and there were so many things I wanted to share with him. Each day, I prepared lunches with enthusiasm. However, he routinely ate them with a lackluster and vacant face.

I call him in my mind. "David … Where are you? What are you doing now?"

After break, the class spreads out and has their own free time in groups. Some children go into a flowing stream, chasing tadpoles and playing in the water; the tadpoles play back, without getting caught.

One attempts to catch a dragonfly sitting on a blade of grass. She holds her breath, reaches out her hands, and is suddenly surprised by the dragonfly staring back at her, rubbing its thin wings. The stunned child drops her hand and looks at the dragonfly curiously as the dragonfly stares back with puzzling eyes. She levels eyes with the dragonfly and smiles innocently.

Other kids gather under the tree after seeing a squirrel. It sits on a tree root and eats nuts with both hands, raises its tail in the air, and cautiously watches its surroundings. The children watching the squirrel wait for it to finish eating while they hold hands. When the squirrel finishes eating, it turns its little head and looks around. The children greet the squirrel, "Hi! Goodbye!", waving their hands.

A father attending a picnic walks along the stream, holding the hand of his young daughter. They catch my attention as they look in each other's eyes, talk kindly, and laugh brightly. The father bows his head down toward her and she raises her head high to meet him. Their affectionate scene reminds me of my father. We used to walk along the river, holding hands, and watching the sunset. My father often told me, "My pretty, Jane! Thank you for being born a daddy's girl."

He adored me and raised me zealously since I was born late. My father told me about many things: flowers, stars, and his life. As a child, I understood all of his stories; I kept them safe without question. As I grew, my father's stories came one by one when I needed them. They made me think and became a textbook of life for me, a message of love. As I look back, I recognize that my father was my first friend.

A girl in a pretty hat walks toward her mother, hands full of wildflowers. The child says, "Mom, the flowers are so pretty! Let's go pick more."

The mother is sitting in the shade of a tree and conversing with other moms. She says apprehensively to the girl, "It looks pretty, but the sunlight is so strong that I will stay in the shade.'

The child walks back to the flower garden alone with a deflated face, unable to understand why her mother did not care about the beautiful flowers.

I thought as I looked at the child walking in disappointment, *When I become a mother, will I also be disinterested in the beauty of flowers and hate the sun? Will the little angel in my heart stay with me if I get old?*

Chapter 7: My Diary of Longing

There is a person living in my heart who occupies more space than my parents. He passed through my life briefly, but in my heart I never forgot him. I still miss him and want to see him again. My sweet memories with him still stir and touch my soul in regret.

He is David, the person my heart can't release. He appeared in my life like a lightning bolt and disappeared like vapor. From the moment I accidentally met him in college, my mind was occupied by him with visions. My eyes were blind to his depressed and rebellious state. My soul sought him incessantly and my hand wrote his name in my notebook hundreds of times.

Soon my dream came true and I met him at a college party. Ever since that night, I fell for and loved him with zest. But my love was not good enough for David. Soon he broke up with me, which brought unbearable torment. After we were separated, I still could not let go of him. I wondered why am I still imprisoned by him? Is it because I truly love him, or is it because I want to be healed? Or is it that I want to make my hopes come true by sharing my lonely, one-sided love with him? Or is it my wish to be compensated for my devotion? Whatever the reason, I realize that the relationship helped me grow.

One day I meet with a friend in a café and we chat, missing our former friends and recalling our college days. Among many unforgettable memories, she talks about the geriatric who used to talk to himself on the street. My friend says, "I sometimes remember the old man who used to hang around campus. He asked us absurd questions and talked about philosophy. At the time, I wasn't interested, but when I think about it now, there was some resonance in his stories."

I reply, "Right! As I think about it, I was relying on him, on Ben, when I was in the bleakest time of my life. Ben always patiently listened to my griefs and aches and eased my hurt. Unfortunately, I can no longer confer with him even though I still have many things I want to deliberate on."

"Right! You and the old guy have been pretty close. He will probably read your heart and think about you in heaven since you made that monument to honor him under his tree. Oh! By the way, I saw David some time ago when

I was passing by campus. He was standing in front of the school lost, like a bum." My friend looks at my face, checks my expression, and quickly changes the subject. "Jane, do you remember Annie, who thought herself the prettiest and acted superior?"

"...Yes... but why? ..."

"Well, she married the son of a wealthy family when we were in school. They divorced in a year. I hear that she is dating several men now. Come to think of it, it's lucky that Annie betrayed David. I think David's love toward her was pure."

"Do you know how David is doing?"

Reflexively, she responds, "His situation is the worst among our college friends."

Quickly she shuts up and glances at me to see whether I am okay. When she confirms that I am still listening attentively, she continues, "You, silly! Do you want to be abandoned by David again? Wake up, girl!"

But, I insist, "Please tell me where he is."

That night, I can't sleep. I stay up thinking about David. I cry, feeling sorry for him because he is going through such a hard time. I scorn my indifference for not looking for him when he lived so close. "David, I'm sorry that I couldn't feel that you are so close to me. I miss you very much."

The next day, unable to concentrate on work, I leave work early and head to the school library. I enter the library with a mixture of excitement and anxiety. I find David reading next to the circulation desk. The moment I see him, I freeze and

the last unforgettable words he spat at me rear up in my mind
—*Thank you for everything. Goodbye!*

I am perplexed; I cannot approach him so I rush out of the library, as I feel my body paralyzing.

I cannot just leave. I sit on the outside bench for a while, calm down and go back inside. He is still looking down, reading a book. As I step toward him, he looks up and around. I panic again as his last words reverberate in my ears -

Thank you for everything. Goodbye!
Thank you for everything. Goodbye!
Thank you for everything. Goodbye!

I do not have the courage to face him, thinking my presence unwelcome. I turn around and rush back outside. Unable to understand my actions, I hesitate for a long time outside the library. *Why can't I approach him? I missed him so much. He is sitting right in front of me*

I am afraid and think, *He may not want to see me.*

I am discouraged. *He didn't love me. He must have forgot about me.*

No matter how much I think, I don't gain the courage or confidence to face him. My heart cries for my stupidity - and yet I am enraptured with the joy of seeing him. I tell myself, "Don't cry!"

I cry for my unrequited love. I return home, appeasing my lonely heart. And as always, I fall asleep longing for him. Ever since seeing David, I feel more alone. My heart burns with apprehension and anxiety.

One day as I am missing the old man, Ben, I visit the campus bench where we shared many stories. On this bench, I talked to him about my first love experience and chaos; Ben spoke about his old and lonely life, amid his hard life.

I sit on the bench, thinking about Ben, the tree, students passing by, and Ben sitting on the bench. I speak to him, "Ben, there are a lot of things I want to discuss with you. I don't know what to do."

I am depressed and sad that we can't meet and contemplate how precious he was to me.

At that moment, I hear a familiar voice, "Jane?"

He once again calls my name, "Are you Jane?"

I raise my head and look at him. "David!!!"

Here he is calling my name! This is not a dream or hallucination! He is calling my name right next to me!

"Wow! It's really you!"

He sits next to me as I tremble.

"It's been a long time. How have you been?"

I can't say anything.

He asks again, "How are you doing?"

I become numb and deaf. I look at the ground, like a fool. He asks cautiously, "Did you know the homeless, old man who used to spend his days on this bench?"

My mouth drops. "Yes."

"Then it must be you who built the memorial for him!"

"Yes."

After a long pause, he speaks again, "He made me think about the meaning of life. I felt very sorry that he passed away so miserably on the street. I had many stories that I wanted to share with him."

The fact that David met and talked with Ben is surprising; the amazement overwhelms me. I stammer, "You mean … you spoke with the old man, Ben?

"Yeah, that's right. Is that his name? Ben? I never asked."

"How do you know him?" I question.

David continues talking as he looks up at the sky. "I saw the old man when I was in school. I ignored and held disdain for him because I saw him asking useless questions to the students passing by. Nevertheless, after I graduated, I met him on the street."

He holds his breath for a moment and heaves a great sigh. After a pregnant pause, he continues talking, but drops. "In the beginning, I was angry at the old man, I mean Ben, who looked like a beggar and I criticized him for no valid reason. But he never counterattacked me with his words. He was always quiet, calm, and warm, accepting my rude behavior. Despite his kindness and consideration, I arrogantly refuted his stories, doubting his life experience and philosophy. Like that, I unilaterally harassed him. However, he was still humble and friendly. Then, as I got to know him better, I was amazed at his humility, his kindness, and politeness. It moved my heart. Since then, I occasionally remember Ben, wanting to meet and talk with him again.

I think, if I meet him now, I can share with him a more mature conversation; unfortunately, I can no longer meet him."

Hearing David's testimony, my heart overwhelms with love and joy for Ben.

I feel that the meeting with Ben and David is my preordained fate. With all my courage and a trembling heart, I cautiously whisper, "David, can I fill Ben's empty spot for you and can you fill the vacant place of Ben for me?

He looks at me with inquisitive eyes, probing my face. I boldly say, looking straight at him, "David, I have a lot of things I want to talk about with Ben, too. Can you listen to my stories on behalf of the old man?"

His dark eyes shine with a gleam of hope, that light shone on me brightly

Part 3: Our Story

Chapter 8: Reunion

(David and Jane reunite on the bench where they first met. It is a pleasant summer day, the blue sky stretching out over campus. Students enjoy the sunlight from the grass field as they read books and chat with friends. Everything is the same as before, except for the awkward atmosphere between the two people sitting on the bench.)

Jane: This bench is where you held an umbrella for me when I sat in the heavy rain, in pain, after we separated.

David: Yes. Although we've changed a lot, this bench is still the same.

Jane: Even though the breakup was painful, through that experience, I think I learned a lot about love and matured as a person.

David: Jane, I'm sorry for my asinine behavior in the past. At the time, I was blinded by my infatuation for Annie and I had no room to appreciate you. After my obsession dissipated, many good memories of you welled up in my heart. You have been on my mind ever since, but I did not have the confidence to look for you while at rock bottom.

Jane: Time has turned our experiences of grief and pain into beautiful memories and maturation. Although my love for you has been lonely and sad, I think it has kept me strong. I have missed you and I am glad that we could meet again. I feel like I'm dreaming!

David: I missed you, too and also wanted to meet. Yet I had no courage because of how pathetic I felt. I hoped that the time would come by chance.

Jane: So how have you been?

David: After graduating I was adrift, unable to adjust to society, unable to find a proper job; I lost value and any meaning to life. Eventually, I became a loser. I was a man lacking bravery because of my broken love with Annie. I wandered in a swamp of humiliation and despair, avoided human relationships, and was insecure in social settings. Life distressed me to the point that I wished to die, not finding any hope in my life.

(Jane wants to hug David and be in his arms. She feels the agony and honesty in his words. David wants to share his past and present situation with her, feeling comfortable in her calm, sincere softness. Their hearts open and they approach one another to embrace souls in a somber hug.)

Jane: So, is Annie entirely out of your life?

David: I am ashamed to say I still see the same hallucinations of her from time to time. I am bitter and disgusted for not being able to completely erase her memory.

Jane: David, can I be frank with you?

David: Please do.

(Jane's eyes are clear and concerned. She guesses David's deepest wound and darkest secret.)

Jane: Aren't you still seeing her because you are imprisoned by your unfulfilled love? Your obsession?

David: Yes. For that reason, I even kill her in my dreams in an attempt to abandon my obsession. When I wake up, I want to die because I feel I have no reason left to live. In truth, I would have stayed with her forever, fooling myself into thinking she was my soulmate. In reality I am disenchanted by the dream. Furthermore, the fact that she left me because of my meager funds and incompetence makes me crazy. I continuously fell into a bottomless despair, questioning what I should live for? I was confused and lost any meaning for my life. That's when the pessimism began and it has been suffocating me ever since.

(David vomits out his deep bitterness. Jane's heart aches to see David's pathetic, wretched state. She shares David's pain and feels jealous of Annie. She despises Annie's mirage that still quakes David's heart. Rather than being disturbed, Jane tells herself to overlook her jealousy, understand him, embrace his soul, lead him from the deep isolation, and reveal to him a new life full of opportunity.)

Chapter 8: Reunion

Jane: You still have many years to live and nobody is trying to take that away. Why would you give up your life? If you perish, your love would as well. Are you not missing her or obsessed because you are alive? Wouldn't you be able to overcome the despair of a broken heart only if you are living? And if you are wondering about reasons for continuing, wouldn't you be able to find the meaning of your life again only if you stay? In my case, when life is so hard that I consider giving up, I think of my mom's death. She died pitifully of cancer. At the end, my mother was hounded by a great fear of death. She struggled to endure and fought against her departure with all her strength until the last moment of breath. I was terrified of watching my mother dying in such a heartbreaking state. Since then, I don't have the fortitude to even imagine death.

David: You remind me of Ben's words regarding death. He said, "Young man, do you think death is a great excuse or simple solution for turning away from this world? At the same time, aren't you afraid of death? Wouldn't it be a pity that you could never see your loved ones again? Don't you have regrets about the dreams that you were not able to achieve in this world?" But Death is my refuge, delusional hiding place, and my own resting space that does not allow anyone's interference. I sometimes think death might be a quick solution for getting out of the suffering from my depressed, distasteful life.

Jane: But what if that refuge is another human life, what then?

David: What do you mean?

Jane: What if we don't die and continue our existence in a circular flow that repeats after death into birth?

David: Circular flow? Eternal circle of life? Do you mean Nietzsche's eternal recurrence or eternal return theory that the universe and all existence has been recurring and will continue to recur through a continual series of cycles? I like and respect Nietzsche's philosophy, but I never thought of linking me, death, and reincarnation. I need to think about your astonishing question.

(David feels like he is meeting again with Ben, who shared philosophy and life. That feeling penetrates his heart with excitement and he is driven to share many untold stories with Jane that he wanted to share with Ben.)

David: Do you think there is another world with life after death?

Jane: I wouldn't know because I haven't died; if I've been dead before I don't remember my past life?

David: If we don't remember death, we may have already experienced it. This is frustrating.

Jane: Many philosophers have said all things in nature endlessly flow in circulation. Then is there any living being that remembers their rebirth? Is it that only humans can't remember recurring phenomena? Or Is it humans who don't understand the cosmic language?

David: Eastern and Western philosophy talk a little bit differently about reincarnation. Buddhism says there is nothing to fear about death because our body and name are an illusion; in fact, we never die, but change our identity again and again. The Tibetan Book of the Dead basically says, "Death will follow birth, and birth will follow death." Bhagavad Gita sums it up with, "As a person puts on new garments, giving up old ones, similarly, the soul accepts new material bodies, giving up the old and useless ones." And Nietzsche emphasized the affirmation of life and encouraged people to cultivate their strong will under the premise that the human soul never dies. What do you think about life after death, Jane?

Jane: Because death cannot be resisted by human power, it seems that we are potentially distracted by preoccupations. Isn't the world after death the imaginary world each of us dream? Don't men wish to live in a world where there is eternal happiness, a sentience without pain or death? And don't we want confirmation of a promised paradise after death, while we are still breathing? However, we don't have confidence in anything we cannot visibly verify. Didn't we search for a cause for our hope and reliance on religion? Isn't religion a means to overcome the anxiety of death and comfort the mind?

David: I guess your reasoning makes sense. I think religion has risen to provide comfort to anxious human hearts. At the center of religion, there is a known fear of fatality. Didn't various doctrines and beliefs, such as repentance, salvation, forgiveness, resurrection, reincarnation, and so on originate from a wish to escape from that fear of death? However, if Nietzsche's eternal recurrence theory or the doctrine of reincarnation is true, I wish I could be reborn into a new life where I can start anew.

Jane: But you haven't even lived this life fully yet. What if you face another challenge in your next life? Are you going to give up again? I believe we just need to have a little faith that we were born with the power of overcoming, the power of will, and the power of creating our ideal life. If there is something great about human beings, we can overcome and become a light by our own will. We are not all alone. There is a larger order that takes care of us.

David: What do you mean by that?

Jane: On the day I buried my mother, I went to the beach on my way home. I sat on the beach and cried until late at night, afraid of being left alone in the world; I was so angry about what had happened to me, so I screamed at the sky. "Why are you doing this to me? What did I do wrong?" I wanted my body to shatter so that I could go with my mom! Even if it was suicide to follow my mother, I thought it was better that than to be left alone without a family. However, I was more afraid of death than being alone. What I truly wished for was that the creator who gave me the breath of life to hear my pitiful story, show mercy, and offer me warm generosity. I cried aloud for a long time and woke up feeling strange. I looked up to the night sky overlaid by clouds. The round moon opened the window of clouds and shined a bright light through the darkness over my head, whispering, "You are not alone." I stopped to choke back tears and wiped them away with my hands, feeling the warm touch of the moonlight in response to my prayer; that experience became the affirmation of my faith. Although that experience could have been a dream or fantasy, it was as real as I was, walking on the clouds holding hands with the moon. But as soon as I woke up from my dream, I thought that it was just weakness or a delusion and I forgot about the incident thinking such a thing can't happen in reality. With a hollow heart, I stood up from the sandy beach and returned home. The next day, I woke up in anguish that now I had to struggle to survive on my own. Finding no hope, no air to breathe, life felt unbearably painful, hopeless, and nauseating. I isolated at home for many days in depression, but I knew I could not be stuck quarantined forever and I started to plan a way to endure. Next, I worked to accept both my fate and the world unconditionally, be positive, accept the inevitable, inhospitable, cold world as reality, and tried to find harmony within. The first thing I did was find a job to take care of mundane matters. As I found work, I discovered a new society and social life I'd never known previously. I began to understand that there are friends who become like family. They care for each other and live in a communal society where they maintain smooth relationships and enjoy the value of life together. As I got used to this society, I became more aware of the importance of relationships with other people and maintaining a social life. Eventually, my mind brightened from the gloomy dark thoughts and found light in life once again. I gradually began to regain vitality and realization blossomed. On that day, low clouds swept across the morning sky; by afternoon, a bank of clouds ravaged the sky, colliding with another, creating thunderstorms. Soon the rain poured down with the lightning. The rain lashed the landscape but eventually stopped and afterward a gleam of sunshine burst through rifts in the steel-gray. A brilliant rainbow spread across the sky. The rainbow that tied heaven and earth with a semicircular arch, like magic, awakened me to the truth of life – The sun is there, even behind the dark clouds! As such, the day of despair and grief will soon pass!—I felt the gentle, warm air flowing through my body and circling; I had a sensation that I was protected and I felt all living things existing around me. As I breathed in the gentle air, I told myself, "Do not be afraid! Jump high with all your might!" Although I tried to live positively, the heartless reality sometimes tests me, suppresses me, and makes me panic; then, I am filled with confusion, discouragement, and doubt.

As David listened to Jane's story, which was like a long novel, David was not bored; instead, David wanted to applaud her courage. She looked like a newborn bird that had just hatched out of its egg, shivering cold in wet feathers. David wanted to soothe her pitiful sorrow.

David: I think I understand the difficult time you went through. However, when I was in trouble, I never felt the presence of nature or the universe, nor did I think that they were moving with me. Once when I took a trip to the mountains, I briefly felt an intimacy with nature. Your words seem to be very easy, but I can't feel them. I want to know more specifically when you feel like being in nature and how you came to believe this.

Jane: David, raise your head and look at the sky. Look at the blue sky and the burning sun in it. The sun rises in the morning and throughout the day it changes its position and shapes until it sets in a distant land. Doesn't everything in the universe rotate around the sun? Don't earth and humans circle that center point along with the planets? Doesn't that mean we belong to the cosmos, existing in the same space, as a member or part?

David: If this land continuously travels along a definite orbit and if my life continues in similar rotation, I want to die freely and be reborn as a new person and take away the stigma of failure.

Jane: David, you are not a failure. You are just crouching to jump higher! And I'd like to tell you that you are a beautiful person as you are now.

David's heart pounds with her unexpected words, which he's never heard. David looks up to the sky to avoid tears. The sky is dyed with the fading pinks of sunset.

David: Jane, how do you want to live in this world?

Jane: Although I am getting old, I always want to be a child at heart and dream like *The Little Prince*. I want to travel and see the beauty of this world as much as I can and love everyone.

David: Love? What is the definition of love to you?

Jane: Faith.

David: Doesn't faith have to be confirmed by substantial evidence?

Jane: No, I'm talking about faith by belief.

David shifts uncomfortably. He takes a deep breath and tries to clear his head of Jane's thoughts that contrast his own.

David: So tell me about the love you feel. I want to hear.

Jane: Among the different types of love that my heart feels, I will tell you of my love for you. After I saw you for the first time, I walked after you as if I were attracted like a magnet. From that day on, I kept thinking, wanting to meet, and know everything about you. But you were not interested in me. I loved you alone. That unrequited love gave me a lot of pain and sadness. Nonetheless that experience provided me with a chance to think, grow, and mature.

David: To me, love is a passionate, sensual feeling. So how can you feel love alone in your heart? Can your love be answered when alone?

Jane: Unrequited love cannot be felt like a sensation of the body but can be felt in the heart. Although I was not able to possess the person I wanted, my love hasn't disappeared because that person still lives in my heart. I think sometimes unrequited love can be more pure since it is often distracted by an ego to control or own another person.

David: Yeah? Where on earth do your endless patience and positive mind come from?

Jane: *Laughs and shrugs.* I don't know.

Glancing at her smile, David feels something from Jane, but is not sure exactly what it is. She is full of faith, selflessness, trust, and devotion. It is the first time that Jane stimulates his subtle feelings. He feels an urge to confess his heart to Jane and listen to her opinion.

David: Jane, can I ask your honest opinion about myself? Although it is shameful to talk about, I formed a habit of avoiding friends and people I know when I was isolated. When I compare myself to others, I feel like a loser. I don't even have a proper job. How do you think I can overcome my inferiority complex?

Jane: David, I believe inferiority complexes are often caused by the result of false perceptions. You need to remove your negative beliefs. Stop comparing yourself to others. I don't think you realize how special and beautiful a person you are. You have gifts that others don't have. In fact, I believe you are more gifted than most. Your road might be bumpier than others, but more exquisite. I believe each person has his or her own distinct allure and character. We just need to recognize our own charm rather than comparing ourselves to others. I think you haven't yet seen your own resplendent contribution.

David: Thank you, Jane, for consoling me. I think you are naturally optimistic when I am pessimistic.

Jane: I think we all have positive and negative sides, just like we all have good and bad in us.

David: Right! In philosophical terms, you are more 'Apollonian,' and I am more 'Dionysian'. When I am annoyed with the world, I can't suppress the urge to destroy everything; so I get drunk, argue, and yell. And if my anger has not subsided, I at least have to throw a stone or something to release my stress. One time, the stone I threw fell back on me, making my forehead bleed. I sometimes wish I could control my destructive behavior better.

Jane: Isn't your destructive behavior a reaction of your body reacting before your heart? There is nothing wrong with it. I believe it is all part of our growing process. It reminds me of Herman Hesse's story, *Demian*—The bird fights its way out of the egg. The egg is the world. Who would be born must first destroy a world.—Isn't it a process of creation of life that, as we grow, we fight ourselves out of the adolescent egg by overcoming the rebellion rising within and transforming into an adult? And through this process of rebellious thoughts and destructive actions in our adolescence, will I not get to know myself better and develop strong autonomy? Don't you think destruction and creation are closely related? Don't you think our destructive emotions are balanced by constructive emotions, like we all have a Dionysian side and an Apollonian side? Isn't creation a progression from destruction? If we turn our attention to nature, we can see it repeating the death and rebirth process. Isn't nature repeating itself, as the leaves fall in the autumn and sprout back in the spring? Don't humans also go through similar processes?

While talking with Jane, David notices that the uncomfortable tension that had been choking him previously has relaxed. His heart swells ecstatically at this opportunity to luxuriate the release of long pent-up coagulated words in his heart. Within him, he begins to break the wall of self-created isolation and smash the prison's iron bar door. The broken wall of self-created isolation has been rebuilt again and again as soon as he began to doubt himself. However, now, he has the courage to overcome his doubts and hinderances. His courage, faith, and self-confidence give him hope for the future. David's takes off the heavy and unpleasant melancholy and begins to walk freely and cheerfully.

David: Would you like to go for a drink?

David says it sincerely. In his heart, he holds Jane's hand.

Jane: That sounds great!

They do not speak any further, their hearts pound with excitement and happiness for a new beginning. They go into a restaurant near the beach and find a seat where they can see the sky and the sea. The moonlight and starlight are illuminating the eatery through the glass windows.

David: What would you like to drink?

Jane: A mojito. Hemingway's favorite drink was a mojito.

David: *Laughs heartily.* Okay. Then I'll take a mojito, too.

David laughs animatedly, feeling exhilarated. It is not the elation of winning a fight, nor is it the destructive contentment from breaking something. It releases great tensions crouching inside him. He speaks in an excited tone, appreciating Jane's cheerful disposition.

David: Hemingway seems to have lived a cool life. I wish I could live like him someday, as a free and natural macho man.

Jane: I believe you can live a cool life! Hemingway is not in this world right now, but aren't you alive right now? You are young with a lot of opportunities ahead. Just live with your natural charm and machismo, which you already have.

As David watches her speak, he finds a new allure to Jane that he had not seen before. He is thrilled with her innocent beauty and her calm, but strong charm. He wants to talk with her more in the future.

David: Jane, if you don't mind, I would like to meet with you more often and share further conversations on philosophy.

As Jane stares at David's freed ecstatic soul, joyful tears spring to her eyes.

Chapter 9: Ben

"Ben, according to the biopsy results you are in the final phase of stomach cancer." The doctor carefully reads the final diagnosis, looking at Ben; Ben sits motionless, mute, and looks into the void.

"How much longer do I have?" Ben asks in a forced, clipped voice full of dismay.

The doctor in charge recommends Ben be hospitalized immediately for an operation; the shocked family desperately asks Ben to follow the doctor's instructions.

Ben is unable to utter a word. Full of uncontrollable thoughts and echoing voices, his forlorn heart weighs heavy. Controlling his tremble, he bows his head deeply and poses countless questions to find any resolution. After a long silence, Ben raises his head to reveal a placid face. Then, holding his wife, daughter, and son, he carefully talks about his mindset. "Can you allow me to make my own choice for my short remaining life? I hope you will allow me to do so."

The family bow their heads and weep, unable to respond. He wants to cry, but calms himself and speaks his decision while holding their hands, "I hope you will allow me to go on my last trip alone. I am sorry. I love you all."

Over the next month, Ben prepares himself to leave on a solo trip by closing his attorney's office, making a will for his family, and purchasing an RV. While he is preparing for the trip, the family continuously begs him to be hospitalized and have the surgery. However, Ben pleads to his family that his honest wish is that he does not want to finish his life in a cold hospital room.

Once prepared and thoroughly anxious, he courageously hugs his beloved wife, son, and daughter, giving them a weak smile. It breaks his heart to think that this might be the last time he holds them. He hurries to leave, not wanting to show his tears and unbearable heartache. As he sees his family crying and waving their hands through the back mirror of the RV, his heart is divided. All he can do is keep on driving. His tears flood out and he collapses over the steering wheel, abandoning himself to the infinite suffering. He cries at having to die and say farewell to his family forever.

On the first night of his trip, he arrives at Shenandoah National Park and falls asleep due to accumulated fatigue.

The next morning, he awakes in an unfamiliar environment, inhaling foreign air, and hearing exotic sounds. Although there is no alarm clock waking him, no TV morning news informing what is happening around the world, no tight schedule to follow, he starts his day in confusion, not knowing what to do first.

After he finishes his continental breakfast, he walks around the camping ground. In the lush forest, birds of various shapes chirp around and the squirrels hurriedly climb up and down the trees. He feels like an alien in an unfamiliar environment. He just stares at everything in numbness. He is standing uneasily on the unfamiliar ground. He paces in the dark, drowned in thoughts and deep sadness.

When the morning wind blows on his face, he feels vigor spreading throughout his body. He inhales a breath deeply once more, feeling serene in the new environment. The fresh breeze uplifts his mood, guiding him through a new world. As he walks he hears the sound of water flowing. Soon, he is greeted by a stream where the surface reflects the sun like a white butterfly.

Ben sits down on a flat rock piled up by the stream. He looks into the stream flowing gently over the pebble bed. The water is transparent, nothing hidden, everything visible as it is. As he watches, an image of a face floats to the surface of the water. That face is laughing proudly with self-confidence and the eyes are full of contentment from a life of debauchery. It is the face of young Ben.

"Congratulations on winning another case! You are the best attorney I've ever worked with!", his associates congratulated Ben's victory at court. He had a private law office where he continued to win every case since he opened. Other people envied his abilities and luck. As his reputation was known in the legal community, his office was filled with clients asking for his expertise, most of them were very influential people. And most of his clients expected Ben to win their cases regardless of what methods he used, even if they were at fault. According to their requests, Ben was able to win cases by finding the opponent's trivial weaknesses and justifying his clients by subtle means and methods. As he gained fame by winning difficult cases, he also gained wealth and began to fall into an illusion that he was invincible.

Ben's proud face on the surface of the water changed into a young face determined with justice and righteousness. "Don't worry! I will let the world know your chagrin and I will reveal the truth! I will do this pro bono since you cannot afford to pay the legal fee!"

The poor and helpless client was thrilled by Ben's good and just mind and bowed his head to his knees. Ben raised him up and encouraged him not to be discouraged, his heart filled with a spirit of righteous service.

Yes, indeed! Ben was a righteous lawyer with a warm heart. He was born into a wealthy family and grew up without wanting for anything. His parents, who were doctors, wished Ben would follow their path and become a doctor, but he, who was deeply humanitarian, wanted to fight for justice. So he entered law school.

He graduated with a perfect GPA. To accomplish his dream, he wanted to gain sufficient experience in a big law firm. So he got a job in a large law office. Armed with the spirits of righteousness and enthusiasm, he reminded himself to practice humanitarianism whenever he met clients.

Soon, his efforts were known in the community and he was truly becoming a just attorney. However, the management of the large law firm criticized his spirit of service and scolded him to charge higher legal fees. Moreover, what made Ben even more amazed was that people were starting to use his good intentions for their selfish reasons. Some who prevailed in their case from Ben's free services were not satisfied with their outcome and demanded to appeal to a higher court for higher rewards. They made rude requests to Ben; some even misused Ben's service to avenge others. Recognizing their endless greed, Ben was disappointed with clients misusing his charity and began to doubt his capability to work toward justice and equity. He came to the conclusion that his dream was only a fantasy and eventually quit the law firm. Yet some people who recognized his excellent skill set still wanted Ben to be their representing lawyer and eventually made him notorious.

Ben's face, which changes from a proud face to a just face on the surface of the water, is now turning into a vulture filled with greed and vanity.

"This is a new limited-edition sports car. It will be released late next year. Shouldn't a VIP like you ride in this level of luxury? It sends an important message to your potential clients. Ha! Ha! Ha!" The auto salesman tried hard to butter up Ben to make the sale, licking his glistening lips. Ben purchased the sports car without hesitation, paying cash. He drove on the highway enjoying the wind and sunshine. Everybody envied his prosperity and ability. Ben reveled in their envy with superiority and satisfaction; he thoroughly adored the life of worldly success, believing that this world was worth living and all his desires could come true.

While he was driving in excitement, a sharp thought slipped into his mind and disrupted his pleasant mood: a fragment of his former image when he fought for equality and justice without discriminating between rich and poor. He shook off the regret and guilt, thinking that *poverty is the sin*, deciding not to think about his naïve past and that his innocence originated from not understanding the cruelty of the real world. He accelerated the car, deciding to forget his past and thoroughly relish his success and wealth. He prayed in his heart, *Almighty God, I thank you for blessing me and I pray for more overflowing, forever blessings!*

He savored his financial success; the money made his life comfortable and gave him self-confidence. Every time he won a trial, his ego grew bigger, and he laughed at his previous foolishness of wanting to work for poor people's justice when he was younger.

Ben's face appreciating the pleasures of life is distorted by a ripple; a face of pain emerges on the surface. On that day, Ben spent the evening with his family since he felt sorry that he hadn't had much time with them because of his busy schedule.

He had dinner with his family at a lavish restaurant. After he returned home, he reviewed the next day's schedule and went to bed. When he went to sleep, he felt a discomfort like indigestion, but he thought it would soon go away like any other time. However a little later, he trembled with unbearable pain, feeling like his intestines were twisted, and vomited from nausea.

The next day, Ben celebrated another victory in court with his associates and employees, clinking wine glasses. Suddenly, Ben lost strength in his body and dropped the wine glass he was holding. He fell to the floor, losing consciousness. He saw himself being carried to an ambulance. He tried hard to concentrate and regain his consciousness. His mind seemed clear, however, he could not move his body. He then realized that he was in a critical state; he closed his eyes and contemplated his condition. While he wandered through his mind, the goddess of fortune appeared in front of him; he exhaled in relief and asked for her salvation. However, the goddess of fortune just stared at him with a cunning smile and coldly turned away. Bewildered, he struggled with his arms and felt a twinge in his stomach.

In the hospital, his body stretched like a corpse and was placed on an MRI machine to diagnose him; doctors examined his body thoroughly using the most advanced medical equipment. Through the MRI scan, they found a tumor in his stomach. They ran a biopsy of the tumor and drew a large quantity of his blood for testing. He felt like he was an animal trapped in a laboratory.

A few days later, he was diagnosed with stomach cancer. On that day when Ben observed the doctor's apologetic expression, he noticed the seriousness of his illness and was perplexed, not knowing how to deal with it. He wanted to know how much time he had left to live. In his mind, he struggled, *What?! I have stomach cancer? But, why? No. No, it can't be! But if it's true, I must die while my mind is still clear. I don't want to look emaciated. But...but...can I take my own life? What should I do?*

No! He didn't want to admit it. He, who occupied the peak of a happy and contented life, never could have foreseen misfortune and misery. He had been confident in everything up to now. Then for the first time in his life, he realized the limits of his abilities. That day was a month ago.

Ben looks into his past reflected in the stream and laments. He sighs and moans, looking at the sky, "Oh, I am sorry! My dazzling and splendid life! You are now preparing a farewell for me. I miss you, goddess of fortune, who has protected me. Oh... you've already left me. Oh, you, goddess of greed and material satisfaction! You have completely toyed with me. My confidence and power, where are you hidden? How can I live life when you have left me behind?"

While reminiscing, the pain comes upon him. He runs toward the RV with all his strength, he pours the painkillers into his mouth with a trembling hand, and he faints.

In sleep, Ben falls into an invisible labyrinth. It isn't land, ocean, nor sky; it is a totally dark space. He sees something blurry in dark smoke. Under his feet, he sees there are countless snakes entangled together. He raises his feet high to avoid stepping on the snakes, but his body is not visible and he floats in the air.

Regardless of his will, he continues to float around a weightless vacuum. Countless skulls laugh at him, ridiculing from all directions, creaking their skeleton bodies, and they run toward him trying to catch him.

Hurried, he floats higher. As he continues wandering through the dark world, he sees burning pits of fire, sewers filled with rotten filth, dim caves filled with bats and cockroaches, and a devil beckoning him into the sea of blood.

He wants to run away from the creepy place and he wishes to find the light.

He sees a place with bright streaks of light. He rushes in that direction with all his might, but is alarmed and tries to stop in haste. There is a sheer cliff. He attempts to control his body, but loses balance, and falls rapidly down the cliff.

When Ben returns to consciousness, he exhales a slow, relieved sigh realizing it was a nightmare. However, he cannot stop the shock and his jaws tremble. He falls sick with a high fever, his body boiling up like a fireball. And he relives the familiar nightmare for days.

A few days later, he regains composure and is bored with nothing to do. He rummages through his bag to find anything to read. He finds a Bible, which his wife put in for him. Since some time ago, his wife had a habit of putting a Bible in his suitcase when he traveled. However, he had never read it during his travels. He misses his wife and opens the book without thought. The moment he opens the cover, he smells the fragrant paper, which puts him in a pleasant mood.

From the first chapter, the story is mysterious and magnificent; however, he feels a sense of distance from reality. Moreover, thinking himself an intellectual, he finds the stories unrealistic and absurd, they seem to be fantasies. But he decides not to read the Bible with suspicious eyes and does not want to search for errors. He thinks people should not read a book if they're going to criticize it because the author's perspective and imagination are different from the reader's.

He just wants to read the Bible like a storybook, not as gospel or dogma, with an open mind. He reads the Bible like his favorite storybooks and finds the plot interesting. In the first chapter of the book of Genesis, the Bible speaks about the beginning of the universe and man and the relationship between both of them and God. The story intrigues and stimulates his interest and introduces Ben to the very beginning of the time.

They say Moses wrote the Bible based on what he actually heard and experienced. But in his mind, he has doubts. *Did such a great event really happen?*

The story is mysterious, and he can't believe it as a 100% true story. At the same time, such magnificent, profound legends couldn't be ignored either. Then, he thinks, *Is my life also related to the beginning of time discussed in the Bible?*

Although he can't fully comprehend what the Bible says, he does not stop, and he continues reading. Then the Bible asks:

"Where were you when I laid the earth's foundation? Tell me, if you understand."

"Hast thou comprehended the earth in its breadth?"

"Do you know the laws of the heavens?"

Ben is dumbfounded with questions he cannot even imagine and his mind goes blank for a while. He drops the Bible on the floor, unnoticed. He sinks into deep contemplation. Many questions come to his mind:

How am I related to the beginning of time?

If I am related to the beginning of the universe, where was I in the beginning?

How much understanding do I have about the laws of heaven?

He wakes up from the void, picks up the Bible, opens it again, and continues reading. While reading the old story, he cannot take his eyes off the book, unfolding in his imagination, drawing many characters in his mind. He is obsessed with reading the old stories for days; it becomes a part of his daily reading. Sometimes, he is so immersed in the story that he forgets his physical pain and can't distinguish night from day.

The Bible stories make him forget loneliness, physical pain, and the passage of time; it makes him think about his existence and life. Eventually, the Bible becomes his companion and a necessity, soothing his aches. During this process, a close bond is created between Ben and the Bible; he feels an intimacy with the Bible. He finds joy in its pages.

As time goes by and Ben moves from place to place, he gets used to traveling alone, scheduling his daily life, and searching for somewhere new. The summer that he starts his journey passes by and fall is nearing; the scenery before his eyes is filled with color and beauty. The wind blows and sweeps the golden leaves on the ground.

It has been such a long time since he felt and realized the beauty of autumn. He remembers that when he was in college, he was an optimist who loved poetry, nature, and romance. However, ever since he started his professional career, he became a secular person who knew how to become successful by winning over others, a computerized person who prefers accuracy and quick responses, and a family man who is committed to doing anything for his family. He was always so busy that he did not have time to appreciate nature or the artistic mood. When he traveled, he only looked for the best hotels with the best facilities. He was not interested in the city's natural scenery. In that way, he has been living in the abundance of the world without feeling the sense of deprivation of the spiritual self. And now, he is a sick and lonely old man. His soul fills with autumn, he walks through the forest, drinking in the cool, thin air of the autumn with rhythmic inhalations. The branches wave their hands as if they are welcoming him, and he greets them with a gentle smile on his face. Even if he cannot communicate through language, he feels familiar and comfortable with the place as if he has come home.

But that happiness is very temporary. Soon the terrible pain attacks Ben's stomach with a fiendish delight in torture. The devil's hand makes its presence known through torture, trying to throw Ben's life into a hell of a death. It yells, "Your life is mine!"

Ben falls on the ground, struggling with the discomfort that is too great to endure, his face smears with suffering and tears. The shadow of death stabs and twists Ben's intestines with its blade, yelling out once more, "Your death is mine!"

Unable to endure the vicious pain, Ben accepts the death approaching; his body sags. His soul separates from his body and is dragged into darkness. There are pitted puddles here and there on the ground, which seem to be made of clay, emitting dark smoke. The red eyeballs flare up in the black smoke as they approach Ben. Ben stares at the fiery circles and resists, arming his mind. He shouts relentlessly, armed with his firm will power as a shield, "My life will belong to the light whether I am alive or dead! It's not yours, you, devil of darkness and suffering!"

Confronted by Ben's strong, soul-glowing will power, those eyes did not dare stare straight at Ben. They lose their poisonous strength, promise to take revenge later in time, and disappear into the dark smoke.

Ben's soul overcomes darkness with its will power and returns to his body. Meanwhile, Ben's body escapes death's penetration by resisting the violent pain with all his might, grabbing the dirt with both hands.

Regaining his body and soul, Ben falls on the ground exhausted. The grief and joy of overcoming his death brings a new flood of tears; he is sad that all he can do is just weep over it. And so weeping he falls asleep; exhaustion and sleep hold him. He sleeps an hour, escaping his misery.

His weeping releases great tension; his body and mind calm to some extent. When he wakes up, he sees a dragonfly through his tear-dried eyelids. It rests on a cattail with its wings folded. Every creature moves along in their best effort to reach and accomplish their destiny in the cycle. Observing the sincere efforts and posture of nature following the flow, Ben also wants to bear some fruit in his life and prepare for a new life that may exist elsewhere, even if the new world, new life, or reincarnation are all illusions.

Midday is stormy so Ben rests on the bed and opens the Bible according to his usual habit. The page he opens talks about the heavenly world described as 'God's Kingdom' and 'Heaven'. Although religious scholars studying and interpreting the Bible explain them in various different doctrines, Ben uniquely and creatively tries to imagine the heavenly kingdom as a third-dimensional, spiritual world. He begins to think that his expectation can be real as he sees in movies and begins to have a different hope he has never felt before. This new hope emerges in Ben's heart and gives comfort to his pathetic and desperate situation. That consolation, although it is hard to believe, tells him what he wants to hear: that this is not the end of his life. The voice that he desperately wants to believe in gives him, who is utterly exhausted, a new hope, joy, and energy. In delight, he shouts to his soul, enduring the pain, "My life! Stay with me a little longer."

With a hope that there may be a new life waiting for him, he wants to look back at himself and wants to learn from his past mistakes. He thinks the best place for him to look back on himself is the college he attended when he was innocent and pure. So he decides to begin a transcontinental trip back toward the west coast. It is a long trip from the east coast, but he is thrilled each day, feeling that he is going back to an innocent time.

Every morning, he opens his eyes with trembling euphoria, hearing the birds chirping outside. He is so unaccustomed to solitude but is now fascinated by nature's sounds, instead of money or fame. Although his changing self does not fit his previous self-image, he is unburdened and free. And he begins to appreciate the beautiful nature of every place he visits and the people he meets during the trip. He feels nature and the people he encounters during the journey are very precious, thinking that he will not meet them again in this lifetime.

On the way to college, Ben stays in the Grand Canyon National Park for a few days. Although he has visited the Grand Canyon many times in the past, he wants to see it once more. He remembers how amazed he was at the Grand Canyon's magnificence when he saw it the first time.

He cannot stop his admiration of the grandiose sight. The first time he looks at the spectacular gorge under his feet, the remarkably incredible scenery is breathtaking. The informational signpost in front of the massive hole in the ground explains that the gorge's horizontal strata were formed two billion years ago. The lines in the canyon show geological evolution through time. Ben can't even imagine how long the two billion years represent when most human lives are less than one hundred years. His body and soul tremble with the breathtaking wonders of nature unfolding before his eyes. This place, the Grand Canyon, shows the structure and changes of the earth's layers. Each segment in varying, distinct colors shows that they were created in different periods and were formed by water in the beginning. The incredible sight leads him to Genesis. "And God said, 'Let the water under the sky be gathered to one place, and let dry ground appear.' And it was so."

Ben is amazed that the grand sight in front of him coincided with what the Bible says, which cannot be confirmed or denied by any research or study up to now. *As the Bible says, was the Earth submerged in water and later the ground was exposed? Who saw the beginning of the time? How can we count the Earth's ages since it began? Who can tell that they were created and are undergoing evolutionary change themselves? Can a person who lives and studies less than 100 years of their lifetime truly explain the beginning of all creation?*

While he is intoxicated by the live scenery, nature reveals secrets through the legend of Genesis. "God blessed them and said to them, "Be fruitful and increase in number; fill the earth and subdue it. Rule over the fish in the sea and the birds in the sky and over every living creature that moves on the ground."

Ben thinks, *Yes! Just as there are my parents who birthed me, there must be someone who created heaven and earth! And each and every thing in the world has their reason for existence. Do all creatures on the Earth exist for humans? Who is the so-called master?*

The natural phenomena in front of him shows Ben the natural world's composition and unity of life and teaches him that the universe, nature, and human beings are interlinked together. He humbles himself in front of the unspoken truth and order of nature they reveal.

A colorful autumn leaves and winter approaches with a cold breeze when Ben arrives at his destination. He finds an RV park near the school and decides to leave his RV there. He walks toward the school campus with a quivering heart; when he sees the café he is familiar with, his heart is thrilled. Like in his old days, a young man wearing torn jeans and rocking long hair is singing and strumming his guitar on the street. Ben sits next to him, singing along with him, feeling unhindered freedom. Now there is no reason for him to be concerned about how people look at him since he knows he no longer looks attractive — his attire is out of fashion, his wrinkled face is covered with a white beard, and his hair is turning gray-white. After seeing his shabby appearance, he feels lighter, realizing that he has finally been freed from his pretense.

Ben buys a cup of coffee at the school's cafeteria and walks up the hillside where he used to love reading books on the bench when he attended school. The bench under the tree still remains there, painted with many memories of the past. They come gushing forth sweetly and movingly. He touches the bench like meeting an old friend, telling the bench that he came a long way to meet it, and begins to talk about his old school days, sinking into a deep nostalgia.

Chapter 10: The Celebration of Youth and Bliss of Aging

As Ben enters the school's front gate, he reads the school motto engraved on the arched iron frame: *Let There Be Light.* Although campus looks lonely and desolate with the winter cold, the sweetness of many memories touches him.

As Ben visits familiar places, he meets his youth, innocence, love, and himself again. When he looks back at himself, he sees his youth had dual and divided natures in one body: one with a bright light and another with shady darkness. Raised in a wealthy, prosperous family without anything lacking, he was an innocent youth, but just like everybody else, in him, there was good and evil. However, there was a greater portion of light than dark in him when he was young that he did not yet know the pride, greed, and ambition for notoriety and honor.

A mixture of many emotions surge in Ben as he retraces his memories of a younger self. He starts talking to his younger self as he sits on the bench where he used to enjoy talking to his inner self. "It's nice to meet you again, my young friend. It's been a long time my pure, young Ben. Please don't be alarmed by this old man before you. Even if you don't like the changes, I came a long way to see you."

Ben mumbles as he looks at his youthful self. The conversation goes back and forth between the present and past Bens.

"I welcome you, my old Ben! Our young days could have been buried here if we hadn't met again. I applaud your courage in coming back to see me. But your fragile appearance breaks my heart, old man."

An eruption of sadness fills Ben's heart. A painful commotion brings a new flood of tears to Ben's eyes and wrinkled cheeks.

"Please stop crying. It is the way with everything; even sadness passes by. From now on, I want to hear the story of your life."

"First, I want to say, young Ben, that I am sorry! I turned your bright light into darkness, as I aged. To get power and fame, I turned your humility into arrogance, snatched your integrity with greed, stole your innocence with shame, and fabricated your truth. But, I did all this for you. I wanted to give you a great life. Please, understand me."

"My old Ben, your efforts have been in vain. I don't want the great gifts you've acquired; they are of no use to me. But I can understand your desire to please. Why are you still crying?"

Ben speaks with tears in his voice, "I am crying because my life was in vain, and I know I'll die soon, unfulfilled. Young Ben, please forgive my foolishness."

"Don't scold yourself! Even if your life might have been in vain, you did not come back to lament, but to find your will for life and your dreams for your future. You are here to find your light. Welcome, Ben, with the old face and boyish spirit!"

Ben visits the bench every day throughout the winter, having conversations with his younger self.

Hastily time flies; it's already two years since Ben first visited campus. Ben is amazed that he is still alive, although he has a wave of pain that shakes him from time to time. It is one of the early summer days after spring speeds by. As usual, Ben spends the day talking to himself on the bench, holding a cup of coffee. At the time, a female student hangs her head as she walks toward the bench. She does not seem to recognize Ben sitting on the bench, in deep thought. She looks very lonely.

Ben quietly rises from the bench, not to disturb her. She sits on the bench, helpless. Ben sits under the tree next to the bench, trying to read a book.

A little while later, Ben looks toward her in surprise, listening to her sob. She hides her face in her hands and violently weeps. Not knowing what to do, Ben approaches her and asks as he hands her his handkerchief, "Young lady, are you okay?"

She stops her breathless weeping and looks at Ben. She says pitifully as he wipes her tears, "Sir, I don't understand myself or my duality at this time. I feel lonely, but another part of me is acting half-heartedly as if nothing happened. I am sad, but the other side is watching me coldly, as if not understanding why."

Ben is somewhat surprised by her words but wants to hear what she has to say. "Lady, I guess you are in love right now."

"Yes, but my love is unrequited love, which came without his consent. If my love is unattainable, what should I do?"

"Could I tell you my opinion, from my experience," Ben questions.

"Yes, please do."

"Love between two persons is either a passionate love together or unrequited love; it provides me a chance to grow spiritually. Love initially brought me exhalation and happiness, made me dream, and opened my eyes to the beauty of stars, flowers, and nature, which I was not interested in before. But love, at the same time, brought me anxiety, panic, and despair. I eventually became so obsessed with love that I became blind and deaf, unable to control myself. However, when my love was breaking and when my loved one wanted to leave, I had to learn how to let go of someone I loved and how to move on with my life. It was a very painful period; but, after the love was over, I began to think about the meaning of our relationship, learn my life lesson, and realize that love helped me to grow and find my will."

"Sir, can I learn something from my one-sided unrequited love also?"

"In my opinion, one-sided love does not create jealousy, obsession, possessiveness, or doubts, which sometimes spoils the true love between two people. Therefore, I believe, although it might be lonely, your unrequited love is beautiful and pure. I hope your pure love will remain in your heart as a beautiful memory."

"Sir, can I keep my torn love as a beautiful memory?"

"Yes, even as time passes by, the love that came to me lives forever in my heart and my soul. Even if the tree seems to be dead in the winter, doesn't it prepare for new life, new sprouts, for the spring? As such, I believe we all move on with our new life."

She pauses to marshal her thoughts while the old man looks at the fresh, lush leaves on the tree. After a pregnant pause, she greets the old man, "Thank you. My name is Jane."

"Nice to meet you. My name is Ben."

Their relationship began this way. Since that day, Ben has cherished each day, keeping all memories in his heart, and prepares for the short remaining time of his life; Jane has overcome the loneliness that made her sad. And Jane often visits Ben at the bench to tell him of her anguish, sharing her lunch; Ben shares with her his battle, agony, glee-his life story.

"Ben, I sometimes wonder why I was born. Where is the beginning of my existence and where is my end? Am I just born in this world as a living organism with a body and die when this body is old? Do I have any freedom of choice on my birth and death? And if I die, will my life disappear like dust in the wind?"

Ben responds, smiling sadly, "Jane, those questions have been bothering me for quite a long time, ever since I got sick and have known that death is approaching."

"I am sorry that I only thought of my situation, not considering your pain."

"Jane, where were you in the beginning?"

Perplexed by the sudden unusual question, Jane flinches. "I can't think back that far, but I believe that God created man."

"Jane, you believe in creationism, then. That's fine. There are different views of the beginning of human life."

Ben takes a long breath and asks Jane, "Where do you think we go when we die?"

Jane continues to speak in a timid voice without confidence. "I'm not sure, but I want to go to the kingdom of God. What about you?"

"As I saw the shadow of death approaching me, I thought a lot about what would happen after. Among many things, I was most curious about where I would go when I die. One night when I was watching the sky, I noticed that the moon, stars, and the earth I stood on moved harmoniously. As I observed the flow of days and nights repeating, I finally realized that I was in the continuous flow of the universe; I realized that I am a part and a function of the whole universe. Since I was born on a revolving earth, I took it for granted that the seasons' change and the universe's movement were natural phenomena. However, as I come close to the time I have to leave earth, I finally realize that there is a connection between my life and the whole universe — I am a part and function of the big universe, an important member of the universe, moving together in one celestial space. And I've come to understand, recognize, and affirm my existence that I am not transient, but infinite like those stars in the universe; my life is not worthless, but precious."

"Ben, what do you mean when you say 'affirmation of your existence'?"

"By recognizing the value and importance of my existence, I've realized that I am an indispensable, imperative part of the whole universe; I affirm all life in heaven and the earth are for me and the Creator's existence. Because I exist on Earth, I appreciate the moon and star movements in the sky and the changes of nature on the Earth. When I exist with all other creatures in the cosmos, am I not also rotating as an essential being in the big space, universe, or larger order? Am I not the function of the rotation of the celestial bodies, the universe, and nature's recurring phenomena? Therefore, am I not connected to nature, the universe, and the creator? Am I not the true activity of the big existence, larger order? And lastly, the place I want to go when I die is where my soul began on the first day of creation, before the beginning of the history of the world; that place is where all entities that exist in heaven and earth start and end. It is where circular journeys of all existence end and meet their starting point again, where everything returns to this oneness. I hope I was there in the beginning with nature, the universe, and the Creator, where everything began."

"Ben, is your dream world in heaven? Is that where you wish to go after this life?"

"Yes. When I was a child, death was not real to me so I was not afraid of it. But, facing the irresistible reality, I began to think about the beginning and the end, because I wanted to face death boldly. By imagining the possibility of the existence of the spiritual world, I became bold facing my death with courage and hope. Jane, my last wish is to go back to my beginning when I die and be reborn with my will power and realization, either in this world or another."

As such, Ben and Jane exchange ideas, overcoming the generation gap. Ben becomes fully accustomed to street life; his hair turns completely gray-white and long. So he ties it in a bun. Nobody who knew him before would recognize him now. Ben spends most of his time talking to himself, walking around campus, holding the Bible in his arms, throwing unexpected questions to students passing by, and sharing stories with students who show interest.

Meanwhile, Jane's graduation comes nearer. A few days before graduation, Jane visits Ben in a more vibrant appearance. "Ben, thank you for everything. You helped me find myself when I was wandering alone and sad. From the heartfelt stories you've told me, I've realized that learning from our everyday life experience is the true philosophy and meaning of life. Even if I graduate and become a new member of society, I don't think I can ever forget your precious stories. Can I still come and talk to you, even after I graduate?"

"Yes, of course. Please, come to see me anytime. I will pray for Jane's new life in society."

Jane visits Ben from time to time even after she graduates, sharing her social life stories.

A while later, Ben feels that his body is no longer supporting his soul. Knowing that death is approaching, he contacts his family and says goodbye. Then he writes a simple memo to Jane and leaves the envelope tied with wildflowers on the bench where they shared their conversations. "Jane, my dear friend. I don't think I can see your bright smile any longer. It's time for me to leave. I thank you for being a friend to an old man who came to find his soul; I will keep your warm heart in my memories forever. I wonder whether we can meet again. I firmly believe we will. Until then, I hope you stay healthy and happy."

Ben says goodbye to the tree, touching each leaf, and says goodbye to the bench, feeling the metal handles; then, he has one last conversation with young Ben.

"Young Ben, I came to say goodbye."

"You don't seem to be sad."

"I'm not."

"Are you really okay? Aren't you afraid of dying?" Young Ben asks.

"No, I'm not afraid anymore," old Ben states proudly.

"If so, that's a good thing. I was worried about you. But how did you overcome your fear of death?"

"The old Ben failed because his life was arrogant, conceited, greedy, hungry for fame and power, and pretentious. I decided that life is endless pain and suffering and regretted my past. But you, young Ben, have provided a chance for the old Ben to find new hope, freedom of the soul, joy of life, and the world's truth. To be more specific, I found myself, my soul, through you. You helped find my innocent self living in my memory and realize that I am not transitory, but an eternal being lasting forever. And you helped me realize that all the vain things, the life of pleasure and greed I've had, were necessary experiences for me to find myself and be reborn again. Moreover, you helped me realize that I am being reborn to love myself, nature, and the universe. Even if all these realizations are an illusion, I feel immense joy in the hope, truth, and freedom that you've led me to see. Therefore, I no longer regret my past but appreciate all the life experiences. Although they might have been vile, contemptuous, and vain, I've gone through my awakening and I am no longer afraid of death because I have hope. If there are kingdoms of hope and despair, kingdoms of heaven and hell, my wish is to pursue the path of light and not lose or forget it after death. Young Ben, although life involves pain and suffering, it was a joyful and valuable experience, and now, I fly into your arms!"

"My dear old Ben! I welcome you!"

Chapter 10: The Celebration of Youth and Bliss of Aging

Chapter 11: Fly High

After David meets Jane and has an opportunity to talk, David's way of thinking changes. He tries to get back into the social circles and live an amicable social life without being constrained by depression. In doing so, he is able to alleviate his rebellious, negative thoughts against the world, get along with people, and find peace. He feels a little awkward with this new way of life, but feels free from the lonely and cramped yoke he was in. So, he tries to change his self-centered attitude and be concerned about other people too in his new life. Winter comes and the school library he used to work for goes into recess for winter break. David leaves for a ski resort to work part-time during vacation. In winter, he enjoys skiing and works as a ski trainer, since he is at an advanced level.

Arriving in the snowy mountains, he settles in a lodge, prepares to be a ski trainer, and checks his schedule. He enjoys working in the wide-open, not constrained by the partition walls. His freed heart swells at this opportunity to work in nature with passion and expectations.

The next day, he leads ski students and works enthusiastically on the slopes. After a day's work, David goes on the gondola to the mountain peak alone. He finds a white kingdom where everything is above the clouds; the nearest mountain peaks look like a crystal kingdom, sparkling and covered in snow. The listless wind swings back and forth over the high, snowy ridges and greets David, creating a blizzard around him. David opens his arms wide and draws a deep breath of icy air. Although his body is freezing, his heart is ecstatic, warm, and comfortable as if he had come home.

He lies down on the snow, spreading his limbs, feeling the warmth of his mother. Heaven, clouds, snow, and wind hold him in their arms and he becomes a snowman. In total silence and tranquility, David feels complete peacefulness, oneness, and harmony with nature. He feels his inner self reconnect with the world. He wants to remember this exhilarating, ecstatic moment, lying on the snow with his head empty, his eyes blank, his mouth open.

He is delighted to see the high wind driving the clouds here and there. David feels like he is a newborn child, lying in the cozy cradle, babbling.

He whispers to himself, "Though I was born naked, I am warm and lack nothing. Though my head is empty, I feel my soul is filled with contentment. At this moment, nothing is lacking. Everything is perfect as there is no more bitterness, regret, obsession, or anger. I am free! Where did this flawless world come from? How did this perfection happen? Did this harmonious world exist in the past? Was it me who did not open my eyes and heart to see the world around me?"

This is the first time he feels the sensation of unity with nature. He looks around as if he is seeing the world for the first time. Everything looks new with his rejuvenated soul. While lying on the snow, David takes out his memo pad and writes a letter to Jane.

> *Jane,*
>
> *I miss you here, in a crystal world, on the mountain's peak. The winter mountain, standing upright firmly in the snowstorm, looks like you. As if this mountain had been here before, you must have been by my side before. Perhaps, you were close to me even before I was born on Earth.*
>
> *After I've met you again, I found a kingdom of light in my heart through you. Your pure and honest eyes made me realize that this world, this life, is precious. Now I can feel the joy of being renewed each day in the winter snow. I feel that my life and my destiny are shaping within me. I want to show you my new and changed self.*

Let's meet when the seasons change.
My Jane, my symbol of will!

Until we meet again,
David

David became a completely different person. Nature changed him; he ended his struggle and allowed himself to move along with nature. What is most astonishing to him is that he is happy with the changes. He finds harmony in his social life by getting along with other people and not comparing himself with others. Whenever he looks back at his past sorrow, ache, and struggle caused by a burning desire and obsession, he feels pitiful and sorry for himself.

David notices aloud, "Everything flows; my past flew away. The past also brings new; a new life is waiting for me. Didn't my past foolishness give me a new awakening, new wisdom? Now, I want to let go of that foolishness, flow freely with the world, and become a better person. I am no longer a wanderer of the earth without any meaning. My life is not a vain dream. My life is a beautiful and wonderful dream. Let's go to the new world with renewed will. Let's go to the world of creation with a new dream. Let's go to the free world with a free spirit."

As the winter ski season is close to the end, David takes his advanced ski club students, who spend every weekend with him during the winter ski season, to the highest mountain peak, the most challenging slope. These students learned many difficult ski skills in the past months and are ready to show off their skills. The harsh wind buzzing at the top of the mountain provokes them in a challenge. Like armed warriors, the trainees stand at the top, facing the gusting wind, ready.

At David's signal, all students sprint at the same time, following David. They confidently maintain their balance, bend their knees and lean forward. As they go down the slope through powder, making smooth 'z' shapes, they look like birds flying low, wings spread. David is thrilled that everybody makes it to the end without falling or giving up. When they finish, they all cheer and embrace David with enthusiasm like soldiers who won the battle against themselves.

That evening, the club members sit around the fireplace, arrange a closing party, and invite David. Until then, their excitement of successfully skiing down the cliff slope has not subsided: telling the different skills they've learned during the season, complimenting each other's skills, and cheering up one another. Then they compliment David by popping champagne, cheering, "David, your ski lesson was excellent! You are the greatest trainer!"

For the first time in his life, he feels worth, satisfaction, and confidence in interpersonal relationships. He shouts, "This is life! Life is worth living! Life is worth sharing! Life is worth opening and caring for each other."

David knows the warmth of human relationships and the true taste of life. David shakes their hands and says, "Thank you, everyone! You guys were great too!"

The winter ski season ends and David comes down the winter mountains and heads home. As he enters the highway, he feels full of the forthcoming spring from trees beginning to bud, brilliant yellow forsythia smiling everywhere, and a wind wafting the spring's gentle smell.

Spring brings new life. When David gets close to home, he is drawn to a park by the colorful flowers that are blooming there. The park wears new light green clothes. David is thrilled to see the amazing phenomena of nature, reborn from the dead.

From the new buds blooming out of the dead branches, David realizes that enduring the hardship in life is to pioneer a new, brighter life. David receives the vitality of spring from the buds; the will power for life that he lost revives within him.

David suddenly is reminded of his whispering voice when he went on the mountain trip alone. And like nature, the earth that he is standing on now also whispers to him, "You! Great, precious human! The 'Light' that created you has made us; we exist for you, the precious humans!"

In response to nature's voice, David says, "Young lives, sing your song! Dance your dance!"

Spring has returned following the flow of the larger order of nature. After David returns, he meets his new days with hope, liveliness, and cheerfulness. On the way to work in the morning, he spontaneously hums along with lightened feet. When he arrives early at work, he cleans, organizes his desk, and makes coffee. The scent of coffee rises like a mist and softens David's mood.

In this way, he starts his first day by beginning a friendly interpersonal conversation with his co-workers. David finds meaning among the people he didn't get along with before. And he learns a philosophy in everyday life — The true philosophy is not only in books but in ordinary life and is always there.

Now, he is able to transform his life from an intense intellectual to a joyous and spontaneous free spirit who loves nature and life.

David and Jane meet again in a park full of spring flowers. The warm spring sunshine embraces the revived mother's warmth, providing the energy of life; the newborns open their mouths wide and imbibe the spring light as mother's milk. A refreshing breeze blows over the light green field and caresses David and Jane's hair. They greet each other with enchanting smiles on their lips, fluttering their hair.

David: How are you?

Jane: I am doing fine. How have you been?

Although it's been a while since they met, they are like lovers who meet every day.

Jane: How was your ski instructor job?

David: It was great!

His dark tanned face looks healthy and his voice tone is energetic.

Jane: You must have worked hard! Your face got tan.

He laughs shyly; Jane is glad to see him look healthy and lively.

David: "Last winter gave me a precious experience; I feel like I was born again in spring. I felt many things in the mountains. The cold winter made me realize the order of larger wisdom in nature. I think, in the past, I only had an artificial understanding of the world and I did not see the deeper indefinable order of nature. I thought nature died in the winter because it looks dead. However, I realized that nature does not die in the winter, but is preparing to be reborn again in the spring. I learned that enduring difficult times is the birth of a stronger will power. The snowy mountain showed me how to overcome and regenerate; I try to apply it to my life. In the past, overcoming was a desire to avoid pain and suffering. However, now I realize that overcoming is not struggling to avoid or run away from difficult situations or tasks but accepting and living out the inevitable experiences of life softly and courageously, trusting myself and the larger order of nature that I will overcome. And the birth of will generated within me is a gift to my life and power to create a new me. Realizing this, I now have a new value for life."

As Jane listens, she sees herself resemble David in his testimonial-like story.

For a long moment, David thinks. Looking at the mountain far away, he shyly says, "The winter mountain was just like you. I missed you."

Jane bows her head, embarrassed; David holds her hand.

It is lunchtime. Jane lays a picnic blanket on the lawn and opens the basket she prepared. The basket is filled with sandwiches and fruits she prepared in the early morning. David gives her a probing look, surprised, and says through laughter, "You prepared all this? It looks good!"

Jane: "I hope you like it."

David begins to eat the sandwich and gives her praise with a thumbs up. "It's so good! It's delicious!"

In his compliment, Jane's heart sings and dances and cheers with joy, soothing her pains from the past.

In her heart, she chants, *David, my first love, my unrequited love, the one who was indifferent to me and who always brought pain in my heart, you now notice my sincerity, show interest in me, and express your affection. I must have been waiting patiently for this day, the day you recognize my love. Welcome, my dear! Thank you, my heart!*

David eats and Jane is happy to see David eating the lunch she prepared. Afterward, the two walk along the shore of the lake. It contains a round picture of the sun and everything around it. The sky and trees reflect radiantly on the surface of the lake.

David opens his mouth as he watches the sky reflect on the docile lake.

David: When I look at the sky, it reminds me of Ben. Where would he be now?

Jane: Perhaps, he is living a new life in the place where his beginning began?

David: Possibly. In fact, when he abruptly asked me, "Where were you in the beginning?" I thought he was crazy. But that question has remained in my mind for a long time and made me think. I contemplate a lot about the meaning of the question; I believe that process has made me become a more mature person. Perhaps, you and Ben were with me in the beginning of the time.

Jane: Then shall we meet again in the beginning of our next life?

A white butterfly drifts in the wind and sits on the petals next to them, like a symbol of Ben. David and Jane solemnly greet it.

The sun is setting; the lake water containing the sun begins to glow yellow. In preparing to end the day, the sun painfully radiates the last golden glow; the lake calmly waits, illuminating in reflected light. All - grass in the field, green sprouts, colorful flowers, David and Jane, the white butterfly reflecting Ben's soul - wait for the sun's majestic ritual.

The white butterfly rests on the petals with its wings folded, spreads its wings, and flies into the yellow-reddish sky. Jane runs along behind the butterfly, raising her arms high in the sky, and mimicking the fluttering. Then she cheers, waving her hands between cherry blossoms and the insect, "Fly high, butterfly, to your dazzling life!"

She, who ran after the bug, looks like a larger butterfly with wings spread. David, filled with the moment's solemn beauty created by lovely Jane, the white butterfly, the glowing lake, and the golden sun. He joins Jane's cheering and running. "My butterfly, Jane! Fly high! Soar high to your dream!"

Jane responds to his cheers. "David who found himself, fly freely and vigorously toward your life! Spread your vibrant wings!"

They raise their hands up in the air, face each other, and cheer together toward the golden sky, "Fly high! Fly high! Soar to the sky!"